GASLIGHT

JE ROWNEY

LITTLE FOX
PUBLISHING

Also by this author

Psychological Thrillers

I Can't Sleep
Other People's Lives

Domestic Suspense

The Woman in the Woods
The Book Swap

For updates, information about future releases and a free book, visit
http://jerowney.com/about-je-rowney

ONE

There are only two explanations for what has been happening. Either he is trying to make me think I'm crazy or he's trying to kill me. The one thing I know for sure is that I need to get out of this house.

After everything that happened here, I should never have come back. I let him talk me into it. I gave up so easily, and for what?

I got myself into this and now, I either get myself out of it or I find out which of the explanations is correct.

TWO

It all started the day I found out that my dad died.

Like any momentous life experience, I remember exactly where I was when I got the call. Mainly because I missed it. I was sitting cross-legged on the lino-floored kitchen area in my crappy studio flat. The kitchenette was barely big enough for me to turn around in, but there I was, head in the cupboard under the sink, butt up against the wall, listening to my phone ringing out in my pocket. Every couple of days the drain would do this thing where the pipe between the sink and wherever the water went decided to loosen and let the grey water spray from the sides of the connection rather than allowing it to go on its way without trashing the inside of the under-sink cupboard. The plumbing was my landlord's responsibility, according to the template tenancy agreement that he had ripped from the internet, and I had signed up to when I moved in three months previously. Keeping the flat from getting wrecked was on me though, so even though I was waiting for him to send a plumber, or more likely to come over and botch the job himself, in the meantime I had to clean up the mess.

DIY was not my strong point, but being a woman in her twenties, living alone, I'd learned how to use Google searches and YouTube tutorials to help me through it. The landlord was useless, and the salary of an agency admin worker was around exactly what you would think it was - peanuts. Don't get me wrong, I wasn't *poor* poor, but I was only a couple of unplanned bills away from there. Do It Yourself was my mantra, not my hobby. Agency work is like a box of chocolates: you never know what you're going to get. What I was getting was a steady flow of placements and a steady, low wage.

My phone chirped in the back pocket of my jeans while my yellow washing up gloves were wrangling with what an image I found on Google called *the trap*. It sounded dramatic, but really it turned out to be the name for a plastic U-shaped loop. It was the third, or was it the fourth, time that I'd gone through the motions with the trap and the slip-nuts (a name more amusing and definitely not as dramatic). Whatever I was doing was only ever going to be effective to a point, but it was the middle of the month, and my pay cheque wasn't due for another sixteen days. You can bet your life I was counting.

I heard the beep as I let the call go to answerphone. Whoever it was could wait. Best-case scenario, it was the landlord, saying he was on the way with his band of merry plumbers. Worst-case scenario, it was the job I had lined up for the following week calling to cancel. Or, of course, it could have been Dan. Even though we'd been messing around together for a few months by then, he wasn't my first thought when my phone rang. I guess we were dating, but if anyone had asked me then whether he was my boyfriend I would probably have said no. If we were a couple, he would have been there fixing my drain for me, wouldn't he? That's the kind of romance I like, and the kind of independent young woman I am. Don't judge me.

It seems strange to think of that now: that we weren't officially a couple when I got the call that changed everything. Looking back, I can see how rushed everything was from that day on. It didn't feel like that at the time, though. Or maybe my situation was so crappy that I was looking for an out, any out.

By the time I was wiping around the inside of the cupboard and peeling the gloves off my red hands, I had almost forgotten about the call. I pushed my knuckles onto the floor to get to my feet and felt the rub of my phone against my butt as I stood.

I needed a shower. Even though I'd managed to screw the relevant parts of the pipework without getting soaked — I was learning more on each attempt — I *felt* dirty. It was only dishwater, and as a ready-meals-for-one type of person, the food waste content was pretty low. There was a certain smell to the under-sink cupboard, though, and I could feel it seeping into my skin. I needed a shower more than I needed to return the call from - I looked at the phone's screen to check - Unknown Caller. Ah, Unknown Caller. One of my best friends. I never answered the phone to anyone if I didn't know who they were, so even if I hadn't been muddling through the sink maintenance, dear Unknown Caller would have found their way to my voicemail.

It felt like a straightforward decision to connect to the voicemail message and listen to it as I stripped on my way to the bathroom. If I had known what the message was going to say, I might have kept my pants on.

I wasn't really listening at first. My brain had switched off, thinking it was another spam caller, and I was singing to myself. Not even a proper song. I was singing that jingle from the Chicken Shack ad. You know, the one with the baby dressed as the chick. They use these cute little images, that fluffy yellow outfit and pink chubby cheeks, when they're trying to sell you the processed meat from their parents' carcasses. Completely normal. "Every day's a Chicken Shack day…"

When I heard the words "PC Dickenson" I stopped, three steps away from the bathroom door, phone in one hand, bra in the other. I'd been swinging it around with burlesque abandon, but I let it slip from my fingers onto the floor. I just about managed to keep my hold on the phone, and felt my muscles overcompensate, gripping more tightly.

"I have some bad news for you, I'm afraid. Could you return my call, quoting reference number 2107276, please?" There was a momentary pause, and I could hear the slightest quiver in his voice as he added, "At your earliest convenience. Please." He gave the number of the local station and hung up.

I knew right then. Before I dialled the digits with a thumb that no longer felt like it belonged to me. Before I heard PC Dickenson asking me if I was at home, did I have anyone with me, and whether I would like to take a seat. They would have been giveaways, but I already knew.

My dad was dead.

I let the officer's words seep in and answered his questions to the best of my knowledge. No, I hadn't heard from him. Not for the past ten years. No, I hadn't been aware of any health issues. No, I didn't want to receive a call from the bereavement services. No, there was no other family. It was just me. I was the last of the line. The Jackson family terminates here. Please disembark and take all your belongings with you.

When I finally hung up, I leant against the wall and let myself slide down to the floor. The lino was sticky against my bare skin, and I felt painfully exposed. It didn't feel that much like a Chicken Shack day anymore.

There were no tears, but I could feel a ball lodged in my throat, like I'd tried to swallow a partly chewed slice of pizza and it was stuck there. I don't know what I had expected to feel when I heard the news, because believe me, I always knew that one day the call would come, but the emotions made my head swim. I don't know how long I sat like that, but slowly the truth began to flow through my body, like the buzz I used to get from the first vodka of the day. The familiar warm, tingling glow filled me, and finally I let the smile break on my face. He was dead; he was finally dead, and I was free.

Or at least I should have been.

I could have walked away, just like I had ten years before.

I could have walked away, but instead, I found myself heading back to Bittersweet Acres.

I would never be free again.

THREE

Two hours after I took the call from PC Dickenson, I was sitting in a small room at the police station. It had very deliberately been designed to look comforting. Instead, the soft sofa and strategically placed box of tissues on the table that was trying hard to appear homely rather than institutional offended me with their faux-compassionate vibes. This was the place where people like me came to hear news like this. The news that started with "I'm sorry", and no doubt for most people, ended with them reaching to take one of the tissues. Not me though, not me.

As the stumpy female officer, not PC Dickenson, but some late evening replacement, ran through the details, I wondered if I should fake tears, try to give her what she expected, just as the room was giving me what it thought *I* wanted. Dan had picked me up and driven me down there and was resting his arm awkwardly around my shoulder. I wanted to shrug him off, but he was doing his best. Everyone was doing their best. I couldn't help it if I was just glad that the old bastard was dead.

I hadn't been through it all with Dan by that point. I'd kind of mentioned that things hadn't been great while I was growing up. When my birthday had come and gone without contact from my parents, I suppose he had to start asking questions. Where was my mum? Dead. My dad? Unfortunately not. Not then. What had happened? There was too much to tell, and two months into not officially dating, I just wasn't ready. I must have told him enough though, because he stopped asking. I'd grown up on a smallholding, on the edge of the moors, with a mother who cared too much and a father who cared too little. It was just another sob story, and in the ten years that had passed since I escaped, I had learned not to think about it any more than that.

That was all about to change.

My mum had left me almost nothing when she died. Everything went to Dad. All that I had of hers was that same red-blonde hair and the kind of skin that's prone to burning if I stay out in the sun for longer than ten minutes. The only physical item I had of hers is a hair clip. Not exactly an impressive legacy. Tiny enamel flowers in a circle, like a wreath. She was wearing it when she died, which might sound terribly morbid, but when Dad placed it in my hand, I grabbed it. I wanted any part of her I could keep hold of. I've worn it every day since. Every single day.

As for Dad himself, I didn't expect him to have left any money behind; he was never one for saving, although I could never tell where he spent what he earned either. I should have been thankful that he was a planner and had paid for a funeral package ahead of time. I was under no delusions that he had done this to spare me the expense. It was more likely that he thought I would leave him in that house to rot rather than spend money on any kind of service for him. He wouldn't have been far wrong.

What he did leave was the house. Bittersweet Acres and everything that came with it was mine.

I didn't want it.

Dependable Dan was with me again, as the administrator of the estate went through the details. It was all paid for: the house, the land, the stable blocks, the chicken barn. Every last part of it was mine.

I sat across the desk in the dark office, listening to the click of the electric heater, trying to think of an appropriate response.

"It will take a few months to finalise the details," the owl-faced official said. "But the house is yours."

"Perhaps some long-lost relative will turn up and claim it," I said, and instantly regretted. I didn't want anything to slow down the process, not because I wanted the house, but because I wanted it finally to be over. I curled my lips into a forced smile to show that I was joking, and the woman nodded her head. I felt Dan give my thigh a tight squeeze with the hand he was resting there, and decided to keep my wise cracks to myself.

"As the sole surviving offspring, with your mother having already passed away, the house would still be passed to you."

She made it sound as though I was the final girl in a mass killing spree. The sole survivor. In a way, I suppose I was.

"That's great," I said. Then, with more strength than it should have taken to summon the words, I said, "I don't want it."

Dan broke in before the administrator had a chance to respond. "Ella!" he yelped. That was all, though. One word filled with shock and surprise.

In the time between the phone call and the meeting with the administrator, there had been plenty of time for me to sketch the outline of my past for Dan. Here and there I had started to fill in some of the detail, but the picture was far from complete.

One evening, a few days after the funeral, I had arrived at his house to find him looking at images of Bittersweet Acres on the internet. Google search was not always on my side. It was only a house, but it felt as though he was looking through my dirtiest nudes. Seeing the dark brick carcass again, even on screen, was enough to turn my gut. I had to lean against the back of his chair to steady myself against the tremble in my legs, and take surreptitious long, deep breaths before I could look again.

The photos on Google Maps showed the place as I remembered it, but it was like I was looking at somewhere I had never been. Despite the nausea, part of my brain had detached the emotional connection I had with that place. We have these subconscious safety mechanisms that kick in after the kind of trauma that I went through. The only sadness I felt was that Dan had gone looking for the traces of the past that I hadn't voluntarily provided.

"This is where you grew up?" he had asked.

I turned away from the screen again in a clear sign it wasn't something I wanted to discuss. "It's where I lived when I was a kid. Sure."

If he were any more emotionally intelligent, he might have picked up that he had done something that had disturbed me, but he seemed oblivious, going on about how he always wanted to live in the country, how lovely it must have been. Almost as though I hadn't told him that growing up had not been like the Chicken Shack advert with the fluffy animals, pastel coloured prettiness, and perfect family life.

When he actually reached out with one forefinger to touch the image on the screen, the one showing the country-style kitchen that was all country and no style, I let out a faint guttural noise I tried desperately to subdue, and left him to his trauma porn. It wasn't that to him, of course, but to me, he was picking over the bones of my past, and clearly enjoying the meat he found there.

We spent the rest of the night watching some movie or another. I don't remember what it was, but the whole time all I could think about was the shadow of Bittersweet Acres, forever hanging over me, darkening my life. When Dan touched me, trying to incite the kind of physical intimacy that had been the norm in our relationship (if that's what we were calling it) up until then, I rested my head against his chest rather than leaning up for the deep, hungry kisses that we were, by then, used to sharing.

Rather than staying over, after the credits had rolled and I could no longer shrug off his advances, I cleaned up and made my excuses. An early morning, a job across town; lies, lies, lies, just to get away and into my own bed. My flat was a shithole, but I felt safe there.

My dreams that night were filled with shadow figures, and the haunted cries of livestock trapped in their barns, desperately trying to break free. I woke with a jarring jolt, my skin sticky with sweat but as cold as the darkness of my dream. At no point had I seen or heard my father, but I knew everything was about him. Him and what he had done.

FOUR

The administrator stepped out of the room, leaving the two of us alone. I felt like I was in a headteacher's office, waiting for them to return with their decision on a punishment. Not that I had ever experienced that. Not that I would ever have dared to step out of line at school.

Dan grabbed my wrist, and I pulled back instinctively. The flash of surprise in his eyes as he let go again gave me a gut sink feeling of guilt.

"Hey," he said, holding up his hands. "Listen, Ella. Stop for a minute. Don't rush into any decisions."

"No." I tried to use my firmest tone. I wasn't going to surrender. There was no way I was going back to that house.

"Please. For me." He gave me that smile that always made the blood rush to my cheeks, and I paused, just long enough for him to talk, just long enough to seal my fate.

I let him place his hand, more gently this time, on mine as he talked.

"I know how you feel about Bittersweet Acres." He hardly knew anything, but I let him carry on without correcting him. I didn't have the energy to go through it all. Not then. "But this is an amazing opportunity for you."

Those were not the two words that I would have chosen.

"I can't," I said.

He continued as though I had remained silent.

"That house, the land, all of it. It's spectacular. Those views... someone would pay a lot of money to live there."

"It's a wreck," I told him, spitting out the last word. The anger that gripped me thinking about how Dad had let Bittersweet Acres rot over the years came out in my bitter tone.

"It's not that bad," he said, but he had never been there when it was something special. He had never seen the sheep in the field, the horses poking their heads out of the half-doors in the stable block. I could hardly remember that myself. "But it could be better."

I raised my eyebrows in an I-told-you-so gesture, and he smiled.

"Ella, you can live in that house for free. It's yours. You own it now. No more dealing with your shitty landlord. No wondering how you're going to make the rent at the end of the month."

That was something. He had me there. But that wasn't enough.

"I can sell it now. I don't care about the money. I'll put it up for auction. I'd never even have to go back there. I… I…" I didn't want him to see me cry, but I couldn't hold back any longer. As the tears bust out of me like blood from a severed limb, Dan wrapped me up in his arms and pulled my head against him, stroking my hair and making soft lulling sounds.

I didn't want to cry because I didn't want him to think that I was crying for my father. I already knew that he wouldn't understand, that he couldn't understand.

"What would your mother have wanted?" He spoke the words into my hair as he nuzzled against me, and at first, only "your mother" filtered into my emotionally charged mind.

"Mum?" I choked through my sobs.

"It was her house too, wasn't it?"

I moved my head slightly, in an almost nod.

"She would want you to do this for her. She would want you to claim back Bittersweet Acres. Make it yours."

Claim back my childhood, I thought, but the words made no sense, so I didn't speak them.

Mum had lived and died in that house, just as Dad had. But while he finally succumbed to his alcoholic decline, she succumbed to him. I know what she did was his fault. I know he robbed her of any chance of a life. Perhaps I did owe it to her to get one over on him at last. To take everything that he wanted to destroy and make it into something – finally – *good*. If I changed Bittersweet Acres, could I change my own history? There was no changing the past, that was for sure, but changing how I felt about it? Getting closure, at last? Perhaps it was worth a try.

I snorted a snotty sob and turned to look at Dan.

"I don't have the money," I said. I was thinking one step ahead of him, and it showed in the confusion on his face. "To make something of Bittersweet Acres. To make it better." I paused, and then corrected myself, "To bring it to life."

"To renovate?" Dan furrowed his eyebrows in the most thoughtful expression I had seen on his face.

Again, my head nodded with great effort, as though fighting against what my brain had started to imagine. A new version of Bittersweet Acres that would erase the one that had haunted my memories and let me finally be free of my father. And Dan was right. My mother had fought for me, and she had fought for her home. Who was I to give it away, or to sell it to the highest bidder just because *He* had infested it with his evil?

I wiped at my eyes with the sleeve of the blouse I had worn for the administrator appointment in an attempt to look like someone who had her shit together. A long shadow of mascara smeared along the cuff.

Dan leaned back in the chair, pushing it onto two legs, and I thought for a split second he was going to overbalance, crack his head on the dull parquet flooring of the office. As I jerked my hand towards him in a useless reflex action that would have been impotent to stop him from falling, he righted himself and let out a long sigh.

"I have an idea," he said.

If I had been thinking more rationally, I might have picked up that his idea – mooted to appear spur of the moment and tentative – had been brewing since we found out about my unwanted inheritance. But I was drained, emotionally, physically and financially, and as he sold me his plan, I thought about my mother.

I thought about the last time I saw her, and how I could do nothing to help her.

I thought about the only way that I could get revenge for her death.

FIVE

Dan's plan was for us to both move into Bittersweet Acres together and use the money we would have been spending on rent to – slowly – do up the house. I wasn't even sure that we were headed towards a committed relationship, never mind one where I was ready to move in with a man for the first time in my adult life, but as I'd sworn never to move back to Bittersweet either, that seemed to be a minor point.

I know how stupid that sounds now, looking back, but at the time I was swept along, straight down the river towards the waterfall ahead. Maybe a whirlpool would be a better metaphor. Either way, I was up the proverbial creek.

I could work agency jobs within a commutable distance, and Dan was more than happy to take the train into the city to carry on with his nine to five in insurance. I only had a vague awareness about what his job entailed, because it sounded terribly boring. If I was getting a share of a property that was going to make me the kind of money that Bittersweet Acres could potentially be worth, I would probably have been willing to commute too, in his position. Was he taking advantage of the situation? It's likely. Was he taking advantage of me? That was the question I should have asked. But I didn't, and just over four months after my father's funeral, we picked up the keys.

If you think I was woefully naïve, consider this: Dan was the first man that had ever treated me with anything like respect. Before him, I had bounced from one place to the next, one job to the next, and one man to the next. Our few weeks of dating/not dating had been the most secure I had been. If we were holding off defining what we had as a relationship, it was probably my fault.

And, you know, my flat was terrible. My income was appalling, and my life was going nowhere. I hated my dad, but once I started to look at the move as a positive – all that talk of it being a form of vengeance for my mum – I tried to focus entirely on that.

We arrived at the gate to Bittersweet Acres with a couple of cases and a car boot filled with boxes. If you've ever moved house by yourself, you'll know that it doesn't take many boxes to fill that space. Dan drove a squat Vauxhall hatchback, and we popped up the parcel shelf to squeeze more of our belongings against the glass of the rear window. Most of the stuff was his. I hadn't taken anything when I left Bittersweet and had hardly gathered any more over the years since. What did I have to show for ten years away? More bitterness than sweetness, that was for sure.

As we drove up the field towards the house – Dad had never bothered to lay a proper gravel drive – I turned to look at Dan, rather than at the looming building before us. I wasn't ready. I half-expected that if I let myself look towards it, I would see Dad standing at the kitchen window, or worse still, two angry shadows facing off again: that familiar family vision I would come home from school to over and over. A recurring nightmare I couldn't wake from because I wasn't asleep.

While these thoughts were pecking at my mind, Dan was focused, staring forward, with an almost smile on his face.

"It's bigger than I expected," he said, when he noticed my gaze.

I didn't know how to respond, so I made a vague "hmm" sound.

"You okay?" he asked, and I realised it was the first time he had bothered to check in with me.

"Uh, you know," I said.

He turned his head, and cast his eyes over me before drawing the car to a stop, there on the hill. I wanted to tell him how dangerous it was. Stopping on the grassy slope was never a good idea. If the ground was too wet, he was going to struggle to get the car moving again. The tyres would spin against the sodden grass and dig deeper and deeper until we would be stuck there. No hope of getting away.

I kept my mouth shut and let him reach across to put his arms around me. He was straining at his seatbelt, trying to hold me while avoiding being pulled back into place.

"It's going to be okay," he said, the awkward position causing his voice to tremble.

"I just…" I spoke. What? What could I tell him that wouldn't spoil the day? There was nothing. "It's a big deal for me," I settled on. "That's all."

I felt like a child in his arms and the irony was not lost on me. Dan was a big man. Tall and broad, a little extra fat on his belly, but in a way that he carried well. I'm a very average five and a half feet, but I felt much smaller next to him. If I had bothered going to a therapist, they would no doubt have made notes about how I chose *that kind of man* for a reason. They may have been right.

"I know, baby," he said, and again I held my tongue as he used that word. I hated it, but I hadn't told him in the early days, and now, now that we were six months into our relationship, it seemed too late to make the point. "This is our new start," he continued, holding me so tightly that I could barely catch breath against his chest. I felt claustrophobic, hemmed in, and powerless, but at that moment, I wanted it. I wanted those feelings, because feeling like that meant that I didn't have space for all the other feelings that threatened to take over.

"This is our future," he said, finally moving back slightly and taking my pale face between his shovel-like hands. His palms on my cheeks, he bent forward and kissed me, his mouth warm against my November-chilled lips.

Bittersweet Acres was my past. A cold, dark past that I had tried for ten years to escape. I finally let myself look up towards the house, to look forwards to see if it could be my future. The black stone shell was no different than I remembered it, but the afternoon sunlight, reflected in the windows across the front of the building, gave a warm orange glow. It was almost as though, without him inside, something had changed.

I caught my breath with a sharp gasp and glanced at Dan to see if he had noticed.

"It looks beautiful," he said. "Just like you."

I was too captivated by the sight ahead to bother to snort at his compliment. I was caught up in the moment, too overwhelmed to remember that the amber light meant caution. I could have stopped at any point before returning to Bittersweet, but despite everything, I kept moving towards it.

Was it inevitable that I would be drawn back? Was I always fated to return? Was I, like my mother and father before me, meant to die there too?

SIX

If getting to the gate and seeing Bittersweet for the first time in ten years freaked me out, that was nothing compared to standing outside the front door again. Actually, it was the only door: a fire-hazard-waiting-to-happen. This house was obviously built before – or with no regard for – building regulations kind of way. Heavy wood, no letterbox, for there was a perky mailbox on an iron spike down the field by the gate. A thought ran through my mind that I should have checked it on the way past. Would people still be sending letters, or, more likely, bills to the house? I made a mental note to walk down later to check. I was thinking about the practicalities and trying not to think about putting the key into the lock and going back inside that house.

My hand quivered as I raised it towards the mortice, and Dan put his onto mine, steadying and reassuring.

"It's yours now, El. He's not here anymore. This is all yours."

I nodded once, but his words weren't enough to make any kind of impact on the petrifying effect of standing in front of Bittersweet Acres again.

"Let me," he said, sliding his fingers through mine and taking the key.

There was no hesitation once he took control. No time for me to stand and question my decisions, no opportunity for me to turn heel and change my mind.

That was my final chance. If I had turned then, before I stepped back over the threshold, back into that mausoleum, things would have been very different. By then, though, the decision had already been made. I had left the bedsit, taken a three-month contract in commutable distance of Bittersweet, and I had made the commitment to Dan. Going back on the first two would have taken effort but were achievable. Dan though? By the time we made it to Bittersweet, we had begun to map out a future together. For someone with a past like mine, that was an immense undertaking. I couldn't do it to him, and I couldn't do it to the part of myself that wanted so desperately to have a normal life. How normal it was to move back to a childhood home haunted by traumatic memories was another question, but every time it raised its head, I bopped it back down like a whack-a-mole.

I'm doing it for Mum, I repeated, like a mantra. *I'm doing it for Mum.*

By then, though, I'd started to understand that I was doing it for myself too. Because I deserved something good to come out of my shitty upbringing and I could make something of this house. I could make something of myself. I didn't have to be defined by what had happened to me anymore.

I had the forethought to get a professional cleaning company to give the place a once-over before we arrived. It seemed an extravagant expense, but I wanted the house to be as clean of him as possible. If I could have hired an exorcist, I would have done that too, just to be sure. Besides, the house had been empty for several months by then, and I expected it to be dusty, dirty and generally fairly disgusting. I couldn't imagine what kind of condition Dad had left it in, either. Even while I was still living there, I'd seen the beginning of neglect and decay. He treated the house the same as he treated his wife and daughter, and it, too, had died around him.

When Dan pushed open the door, though, there were no traces of that rot. A faint scent of bleach, masked by a decent, not unpleasant, lemon aroma emanated from the hallway. The doors that I knew led through into the living room and kitchen were closed, so the only light entering the hall was through the door we had just opened. Our two shadows ran before us into the house, long, thin and clearly more confident that I.

Rather than flicking the light on, I gave Dan one quick glance, a tiny nod, and then stepped forward to push open the living room door. I used the word mausoleum before, but looking into that space felt more like entering a museum. The artefacts of my past life, for the most part preserved, just as I remembered them. I wasn't sure it was a good thing.

Dan had suggested that we hired a company to clear out the furniture and order new before moving in, but in reality, it was an expense that neither of us could afford. So, there they were, the sofa and armchairs that I had sat upon, bounced upon, and slept upon at times during my childhood. I could almost picture Dad sitting in the armchair nearest to the window, and Mum patting the soft brown seat next to her on the sofa.

Come in love. It's nearly time for Corrie.

She loved watching her soaps, and I loved being next to her. This thought alone pushed a smile to my lips, a smile I never expected to feel on walking back into that room. I had built myself up for flashbacks of stormy rages, brought to bear on mostly Mum, sometimes me. Mostly Mum, though. Mostly Mum.

"You okay?" It had become Dan's most frequently asked question. I don't know what he would have done if I had turned to him and said, "No, actually."

"I'm… okay," I said, spacing the words, dreamlike, as I walked into the room and pulled the curtains wide.

The unpleasant memories ran through Bittersweet, but just like its name, the good were intermingled with the bad. Everything I had of Mum was embedded in that house.

I looked back to the sofa, half-expecting to see her sitting there, beckoning me over, and I flopped down onto that same cushion that had been my place for so many years. When I looked to where she would have sat, though, there was nothing. I could only see past that space, to the open curtains and the bars on the window beyond.

SEVEN

Over the next couple of days, we began to slip into a rhythm without either of us noticing. In the morning Dan drove us to the small village station, where he took the train into the city, and I got off two stops before him and head to my placement. I'd been lucky to pick up a three-month posting in a fitness club. Mostly data entry and answering the phone, but it was low-effort, and the stability of a longer assignment was more attractive to me then than it had ever been before. Before I moved back to Bittersweet, I started to get itchy feet if I stayed anywhere – or with anyone – for too long. I credited Dan with bringing about that change in me, but maybe it was the thought of doing my mum proud that was motivating me. Not just through reinvigorating Bittersweet, but by reinvigorating myself. Just as the house and land had been left to deteriorate, I had let myself fester too.

Dan vowed he would start to chip away at the jobs that needed doing around Bittersweet when the next weekend came, and there were a lot of jobs that needed to be done. I could see our future already: the day-in-day-out drudge of work punctuated by Saturdays and Sundays taken up by fixing, fastening, and refurbishing. The livestock was long gone, but the animal houses were still standing, just about. The feed shed had lost a panel from its corrugated roof. One of the doors on the stable block was hanging, flapping like a loose tooth. Dan was methodological, cataloguing tasks to be completed, work to be done, and prioritising the load. What he couldn't do himself, we would have to save up for.

Everything was going to take time, but I thought we had plenty of that.

I had a few priorities of my own. The bars on the windows would have to go. That was close to the top of the list. When Dan had asked me about them, I mumbled something about them being for security, but it was a lie, and I knew it. If the roles were reversed, I would have dug deeper, tried to find out more about what had happened to the person I had committed to living with in the house we had committed to living in together. Instead, he accepted everything I said at face value. He trusted my word, and I bristled at his unwillingness to unpick the truth of me.

I never expected that it would be easy, sleeping in the bed that had once belonged to my parents. As a child, even their bedroom had been off-limits to me. I don't recall ever being told that I wasn't allowed to enter, but the door was always closed. Even opening it the tiniest crack to peek inside and see if either of them were awake in the morning felt like a punishable offence, and that was the last thing I wanted. Sleeping in their bed, even when both of them were dead and gone, was like lying down on their graves.

Unsurprisingly, I lay awake long past the time when Dan kissed me goodnight, shimmied over and fell, almost immediately, asleep. I was alone with my own thoughts for hours at a time, until my overtired brain gave up the fight and finally let me drift into a shallow, unsettled sleep.

It was on the third night that things began to fall apart.

I'd been staring at the shadows on the ceiling for an hour and a half. Beside me,

Dan was motionless, apart from the rise and fall of his chest. Somewhere in that space between awake and asleep, I heard a soft thudding sound from the landing. There were three rooms on the upper floor: the bathroom, the bedroom I had slept in as a child and the room in which I was lying awake. The landing, wooden-floored and empty, ran between them and on to the stairway to the lower floor. But if it was empty, what was making the noise?

I held my breath, trying to focus my ears on the sound. It had the timbre of footsteps, padding along, coming closer, almost like what Mum and Dad would have heard from their room when I was a child, walking to them through the darkness.

The house was secure, of that I was certain. Much as I despised the window bars, they gave me the security that nobody could break into Bittersweet. The front (only) door was solid and dead bolted. There was no other way in.

I strained to listen, but the noise stopped almost as suddenly as it began.

Of course, I was bound to be on edge. I knew that. Back at Bittersweet Acres, sleeping in my dead parents' bed; it's not what sweet dreams are made of.

Go to sleep, Ella, I muttered to myself, loudly enough that I would pay attention to my own command, but quietly enough not to wake Dan.

I rolled onto my side, facing towards him. The outside world was the kind of dark that you can only see in places like Bittersweet, distant from the background light of the city. The sky was clear and unpolluted. It was one of the few things I had missed after leaving as a teenager. At Bittersweet Acres, the stars were sharp and clear. The night was velvet blue right down to the horizon. The shadow shape of the bars was just discernible through the curtains.

Pad, pad, pad.

The noise came again from behind me, and I wished I hadn't turned around. If someone burst through the door, I wanted to be able to see them. I wanted to be ready. For what, though? What would I do if there was someone there?

There's nobody here. My inner voice was almost angry at my overanxious imagination.

But the sound continued. A tapping of feet all the way along the landing, from one bedroom to the other. So if someone *was* there, they were right outside the door.

I had been wrong before, when I thought the footsteps sounded like those that child-me would have made. This padding was heavier, the pacing longer. It was the sound of an adult.

Pad, pad, pad.

I was holding my breath, trying not to make any sound that would stop me from hearing whatever was happening in the hall, trying not to be heard by whoever was there.

Had someone been squatting in the house while it was unoccupied? Had we checked everywhere before settling down into our new home? I'd read stories on the internet where people had been hiding out in the loft space or ducking into cupboards, only to come out when the homeowners were asleep to take their turn at inhabiting the house.

No one could get in, I told myself.

I could almost hear my dad's voice as we watched the last of the barred window frames being fitted.

"I'll keep you safe," he said, but we knew he meant just the opposite.

I let myself exhale, as softly as I could manage, and tried to settle my breathing. I had to concentrate on what should have been coming naturally to me. My lungs had forgotten that they were meant to inflate, deflate, repeat. My entire body, inside and out, was in stasis. If I kept still, if I kept very still, I would be left alone.

That thought sent a shudder through me. I knew it was an echo of a thought long ago, but I didn't want to spend any more time reflecting on it. There was enough to think about without that.

Pad, pad, pad.

There was something strange about the noise. I couldn't work out what it was. Not just that it shouldn't have been there, that nobody could be in the house, but there was something else.

"Dan!" I started with a loud whisper.

"Dan!" I repeated, increasing the volume, when the whisper didn't have an effect.

Pad, pad, pad.

"Dan!" I reached over and placed my hand on his chest, pressing lightly in an attempt to wake him as gently as possible.

"Ugh." He let out a spluttering cough, undoing all the good work I had done in keeping quiet. Still, his eyes were closed.

"Dan," I said, back to using my regular voice. "Dan, I can hear something. Dan."

I don't know why I thought that repeating his name would have any kind of effect, but apparently it worked. With great effort, he opened his eyes and looked at me. For a split second, that is, before he turned his gaze past me to the glowing face of my phone.

"It's half-past three, El. What's the matter?"

His voice was gravelly and filled with irritation.

"I'm sorry," I said. "But I heard something. I…" What? I'm scared? Confused? "I don't know what it is."

"Ugh?" he asked.

"A noise. It sounded like… like footsteps. I thought, I mean, I think there might be someone out there."

I wasn't sure what I thought, but I didn't know what else to tell him.

Dan didn't reply, and when I moved my lips to talk again, he made a shushing noise. It took me a couple of seconds to realise that he was listening, trying to hear what I had heard. We both lay in silence beside each other, waiting for that sound. I wanted it to be gone, of course, or for it to have been nothing. But at the same time, I wanted him to hear it, to tell me it was the heating pipes or a bird on the roof, or any kind of explanation that I wouldn't accept but that at least would let me know that there was a noise, and it didn't only exist in my mind.

There was nothing.

"Can you still hear it?" he asked, after we had lain there for a long minute.

The fact that he asked the question abashed me. Did he not believe I had heard something, or did he think I was still hearing it, even though he clearly was not?

"No," I said, trying to subdue my feelings. "No, it's stopped now."

"Good," he said, rolling to face away from me. "Night then, El. Try to sleep."

Like it was that easy.

For him, apparently, it was.

Within minutes his breathing changed to the slow in and out of sleep, while I lay, looking at the freckle constellations on his back. Dark stars on a shadow sky.

I heard the padding again, but this time, only echoed within my mind.

As I finally drifted towards sleep, the realisation struck me, and I jolted back awake.

I understood what was strange about the sound.

The padding footsteps were coming towards this bedroom door. Each time I had heard them, they were getting closer. There was no return journey, no walking back to the other bedroom. The steps began there and ended here in a one-way trip.

My breath caught in my throat at the impossibility of it, but I knew I was right.

Whoever, or whatever, had made the sound had been coming towards me.

Always towards me.

EIGHT

The following day, I tossed the question around in my head: *should I talk to Dan about the noise last night?*

Part of me wanted the reassurance of knowing I wasn't alone and that the noise hadn't been a figment of my stressed imagination. Part of me wanted to remain beneath the radar; I didn't want Dan to think I was unhinged. The truth was, I was insecure in the relationship. Not because of anything he had said or done; he had been nothing but supportive since we became more serious. I knew my insecurity was rooted deep within me, in my own personal history and experiences. In the way that I had never seen what a positive, supportive relationship was before.

That evening, after dinner, in the quiet time that we spent settled on the sofa that Mum and I used to share, I tried to find a way to address my fears that didn't make me seem irrational. I decided to put it to him as a general concern about security, give him something to do as a loving, caring, normal partner.

I'd been building myself up to asking, but I tried to make myself sound as casual as possible.

"Do you think you could just, er, have a check around? Make sure that we're safe here? I mean, this house is pretty remote."

Bittersweet was far enough from the nearest houses that the broadband company had refused to supply cable to my parents unless they paid a five-figure sum. I whined about that, as a teenager, but for Mum and Dad, it seemed like a validation of the house's unique worth. They wanted the distance and isolation.

"Sure," Dan said with a sigh in his tone that let me know his efforts were going to be half-hearted.

I tilted my head towards him, trying to read his expression, but he was blank.

"I said I'll do it, okay?" he said. His voice was that of someone trying to be reassuring, but the reluctance was undeniable.

I chose to let it go.

"Thanks, Dan."

It was already dark outside, and the two of us were cocooned within the house, warm together against the winter cold. To the outside world, we would have looked like a happy couple, curled beneath a blanket, watching crappy evening television, living a regular, uncomplicated life. If I let go of my anxieties, perhaps I could believe that too, but everything reminded me of my past. Instead of settling into a cosy, comfortable relationship in our home together, I was ruining everything.

A tear rolled down my cheek, and I tried to ignore it. He wasn't going to notice one silent tear. I could hide my grief; I didn't need to pollute our evening with my sadness. But the single tear became a steady stream, and the stream flooded into a deluge. Before I had any chance of holding back, I had pressed my head into Dan's chest, hacking out body-shaking sobs.

I could feel his hand hovering over my back before he laid it upon me, in what felt like a hesitant embrace.

"Oh no, El," he said. "Don't. Please."

He sounded more impatient than reassuring, and it did nothing to help the situation. Don't. As if I could stop. As if I were crying on purpose, just to piss him off.

Still, I apologised.

"Sorry, Dan," I hacked through my tears. "I'm so sorry."

And I was. I knew I wasn't exactly giving him the best start to our cohabiting relationship, but we were there, in that house, and that had really been his choice. He wanted me to take Bittersweet. He wanted me to move back there. Wasn't he at least in part to blame for how I was feeling?

"It's fine," he said in a tone that made me feel the opposite was true. "I mean, it's understandable. It must be strange for you. You're bound to be unsettled, right?"

"Uh huh," I said, trying to control my breathing and pull myself together.

"You haven't been sleeping well. You're over-tired. Do you think perhaps you could visit the doctor? Maybe get some help?"

"Help?" The only help I wanted was for him to let me know we were alone in the house. Or confirm it for me. What other help was there?

"Sleeping tablets or something? I don't know. What do you think you need? Something for anxiety? Is that what it is?"

I could tell he was trying to be helpful, but it felt like an attack.

I was being overly defensive. Probably because he was right; I was anxious, and sleep deprived.

I tried to keep calm as I replied.

The tears had stopped, at least.

"Maybe we should leave it to the doctor to diagnose me," I said, with more venom than I had intended.

"Sure, whatever," he said, unravelling his arms from around me, and drawing back.

The pair of us sat in silence, staring at the television but not really watching, until eventually I spoke.

"Those noises I heard last night. I didn't want to wake you but..." I looked at him to check he was listening. "I was scared." When he didn't reply, I decided to keep talking. "I was worried in case someone was... you know..."

"I'll check around the house, okay?" he said, abruptly. "But there's no one here. Your dad did a great job with those bars, and the front door is..."

"Solid, I know. But I did hear something. Like footsteps."

"It was probably the heating clattering away. The pipes, something like that." He turned to look at me then. "Or a ghost. Is that what you think it is?"

I shook my head. "No. Of course not. I mean… no. It couldn't be."

"Oh, come on," he said. "You don't believe in all that?"

"No," I said again. There had been times over the years since Mum had died that I wished ghosts existed. I would have given anything to see her again, to talk to her, to find out for sure what happened. If ghosts were real, she would have come back to me. "No."

"Okay, good," he said. And then, softening, he repeated his reassurance. "I'll check around the house. But I think you should call in to the doctor's. I'm worried about you."

To be honest, I was worried about myself too.

I was right to be, but I was worrying for the wrong reasons. If I had known then, perhaps everything would have been different.

NINE

The village surgery was built on the old car park behind the fish and chip shop, and had gradually grown over the years. The GP, Doctor Wilson, and the surgery only had the one doctor, had known me since before I was born. He cared for my mum when I was still inside her pregnant belly and saw me throughout every childhood illness and injury. When I had appendicitis, it was Doctor Wilson that made a house call, racing me to hospital in his red Volvo because he knew it would be quicker than calling out the ambulance from the other side of the city. When Mum died, he personally called me in and sat with me in silence until I could finally speak. Ten years on, I was surprised but grateful that he was still in practice.

Still, making an appointment to see him felt like I was showing my weakness to the world. If I hadn't been prepared for how moving back to Bittersweet would make me feel, surely I shouldn't have done it. I couldn't expect Doctor Wilson to solve everything, just like I couldn't ask that of

Dan, either. But Dan was right. I was exhausted, emotional and stressed enough to be losing sleep and still hearing those noises.

I booked myself in.

In the decade that had passed since I last saw him, I had grown from a sullen teenaged girl into a cynical, introverted adult. Doctor Wilson, on the other hand, had barely changed at all. He sat at his desk in what could even have been the same tweed suit that I had seen him in just before I left Bittersweet as an eighteen-year-old and greeted me with the same perfectly white-toothed smile.

"Well, if it isn't little Ellie," Doctor Wilson said, leaning to shake my hand.

No matter how many times my mum had corrected him, and with no regard for the name on the patient notes on his screen, he would not be corrected. I didn't mind, though. I had never minded.

"Doctor Wilson," I said, complying with the shake. "Hi."

My greeting was sheepish and unsure. Me, back here, back in his surgery, back at

53

Bittersweet. I couldn't help but speculate over what he must think of me.

"Didn't expect to be seeing you," he said. "Although there has been talk in the village, you know how it is. They said you were home."

Home. Was that what this was? A homecoming? It felt more like a retaking.

When I became lost in my thoughts rather than responding, he continued.

"Well, anyway." He cleared his throat and turned to look at his screen, as though trying to maintain a professional rather than curious front. "What can I do for you?"

I'd had time to think about what I wanted to tell and what I wanted to keep to myself. I needed help sleeping. That was the goal, so I stuck to the indisputable facts.

"I'm having trouble getting to sleep," I said. "I know it's probably to be expected, you know, considering."

He nodded at that, and watched, waiting for me to say more.

"Can you help? I mean, can I get something to help me sleep?"

"Well, I don't like to prescribe pills for that kind of thing," the old man apologised.

"Chances are if you leave it a few days, settle in to your new – old – home, I'm not sure which you'd call it now, well, I think you'll find that this problem might go away on its own. How long have you been back?"

I told him, although I could see that he had already made up his mind.

I had distinctly heard footsteps on the landing, but I knew there couldn't be anyone there. It was impossible, yet the sound was so real. I couldn't tell him. I couldn't. For a moment, sitting in front of him, I wondered if Mum had come here too, and sat in the same chair, holding back her own truths.

If she'd ever reached out for help, it wasn't to me.

"It's bound to be difficult for you," he said, not clarifying whether he meant moving house, or facing up the ghosts of my past.

"Okay," I replied, although nothing was really okay.

He caught the disappointed look on my face and shifted his attention from the screen towards me.

"Oh Ellie," he said, his voice reminding me of the way he used to speak to me when

I was a child. "I want to help you, but for now, the best you can do is give it some time. The last thing you want is to develop a need for sleeping pills."

It sounded terribly informal, but at least he didn't use the word *addiction*. It would have been true, though. The last thing I wanted was to develop another addiction. It had only been a couple of years since I had ditched the vodka breakfasts, and there was no way I needed to replace one crutch with another. I had learned to walk on my own two feet, and I knew he was right, on some level, that I should try to get through my dilemma-of-the-day without developing a dependence.

So I nodded, and breathed a quiet, "You're right."

Just for a little while? my inner addict piped up.

I pushed the thought back down.

"Is there anything I can do?" I asked the doctor.

"Give it some time," he repeated. "If there's no change in a couple of weeks, come back and let's talk about it again. Alright?"

A couple of weeks. It wasn't a long time.

I could get through a couple of weeks of broken sleep and anxiety, if it continued. And if everything settled into place during that time, I would have avoided the drugs. That had to be a good thing.

A couple of weeks was nothing.

What I didn't know then was that things would spiral out of control before I made it through those two weeks.

In less that two weeks, I would be trapped in Bittersweet Acres, fighting to escape.

Fighting for my life.

TEN

If I let my rational mind take over, I could find explanations for the noises on the landing. For one, I knew that there couldn't really be a person out there. That was simply impossible once I knew Dan had checked everywhere in the house. I was insistent about all the ridiculous places that I asked him to look into. He drew the line at removing the bath panel and checking in the space below the tub, but apart from that he humoured me, moving aside the mops and brooms in the store closet, shining the torch from his mobile phone beneath the beds in the spare room (my room) and ours. There was nobody else in the house.

That said, the noises didn't stop.

The noises didn't stop, and I was still awake at three in the morning to hear them.

My thoughts kept my sleep-deprived brain occupied in those early hours. I heard the echo of Doctor Wilson's advice: *Give it some time*.

I was trying my best, but each time I heard that *pad, pad, pad*, my heart raced, and each time I thought it might be the moment that a hand reached out onto the doorknob and someone or something would burst into our room.

What I did decide to do, on the third night of hearing the padding, was to steel myself to get out of bed and see if I could catch sight of anything out there on the landing that could have been making the noise. I lay awake, as I had become accustomed to doing, this time hoping that I would hear the sound. Half-hoping, anyway, because although I had mentally made the decision that I was going to fling the door open and catch the culprit in the act, I was also terrified about what I might find.

My rational mind knew that there was nobody there.

My rational mind knew that there were no such thing as ghosts.

My rational mind knew that every night I heard footsteps outside my bedroom door.

And so I waited, almost holding my breath so I could hear that noise when it inevitably came. There was no fear that I was going to fall asleep; half-past two was way too early for that luxury. I waited, feeling the soft movement of Dan's sleeping body beside me, wondering if I should have warned him about what I planned to do.

If, impossibly, there was someone or something there, I was going to need Dan. A fragile nine stone woman, with no muscle and no moves, was nowhere near as fierce an opponent as her towering, bulky partner. Dan looks more fearsome than he actually is, and I would never have thought that he was the fighting type. But really, I still didn't know him all that well.

I was considering tapping him gently on the shoulder, waking him, and explaining what I was going to do when I heard the first *pad.*

Drawing the duvet back as quietly as I could manage, I slipped from beneath it and set my feet on the carpeted floor. My breathing was too loud, even though I was already controlling my inhalations and exhalations, and I took a quiet gasp and held it in. This wasn't going to take long; I needed every advantage I could.

Despite having the heating on in the house, and the fact that I was wearing my unattractive red tartan pyjamas, my skin was clammy, and the chill brought goose pimples to my flesh. I would have rubbed at my arms, brought some heat to them, but I couldn't risk any additional noise. I had to be stealthy; I had to catch the intruder unaware.

I reached my hand out towards the door handle and paused, only an inch away, looking at the round knob, while my heart pounded out of my chest. The *pad, pad, pad* was repeating, and I could hear it clearer, now I was closer to the door.

The breath I was holding caught in my throat and threatened to choke me. I wanted desperately to cough, but I held back. My rational mind was letting me down. A flash of images — potential scenarios — ran through my mind. There was someone there. A man, waiting for me to open the door before he pounced. An animal, something large and ferocious, although in my thoughts it was a smear of sharp white teeth and dark velvet fur; a hellhound more than anything real. A ghost. A ghost. A ghost. My dad, coming for me, ready to grab hold of me, yell in my face, ask me what the hell I thought I was doing back there, in his house, in his bedroom, in his bed. What I thought I was doing going back there at all.

Tears were stinging my eyes, and I had to pull my hand back from the door to wipe them away. I wanted – needed – my vision to be clear. When I moved my arm forward again, my sight was drawn to the backplate of the knob. That was another of those words I had picked up from YouTube DIY videos back in my shabby bedsit: backplate. I'd had to change the lock there, when the landlord had decided that it was perfectly fine to turn up unannounced and use his key to come into my flat. I won't tell you what I was doing when he walked in, but I wasn't alone, and I wasn't dressed. To avoid any further inconvenient, illegal visits, I picked up a new lock and switched them over: knob, backplate, spindle, and all.

The backplate on my parents' – my – bedroom door, dating back to the peak of my father's home security phase, had a small mortice lock. Instead of pulling on the handle, I lowered myself to the floor and knelt beside it, trying my best not to make any additional creaking sounds. I needed time to compose myself, but I didn't want to miss the window of opportunity. The padding was thudding down the landing, always towards me, and I had to look.

I had to make myself look.

I leant forwards, moving my eye towards the aperture, hoping that there would be enough light in the upstairs hallway so that I could see what was there, and hoping that there was nothing there at all.

Putting a hand against the wood to steady myself, I closed my left eye and pressed my right to the metal, peering into the shadowy beyond.

Pad, pad, pad.

The sound came on cue, and my frantic mind was almost convinced that it was faster that time. Whatever was creating the padding could sense that I was there, and it wanted me gone.

Well, whatever was making that sound, I couldn't see it. The landing was indeed dark, but not so much that I couldn't make out the shape of the rail to the right, and the doors to the bathroom and second bedroom on the right. If there had been anyone or anything out there, I would have seen them.

Pad, pad, pad.

As I had my face against the door, the noise came again. I swayed slightly, almost tipping backwards and falling back into the bedroom with a thud. I steadied myself in time, putting my hands awkwardly out to my sides, and twisting my wrist in the process. I would normally have barked out a choice expletive, but then, perched at the door, I held it back, mentally trying to subdue the pain.

Even as I heard the padding, I could see nothing.

Maybe it's an invisible *ghost?*

My imagination was clutching at straws, and I knew it. The fact of it was that there was nothing there. Whatever was making the sound, I couldn't see it.

I pushed back from the door, got to my feet, and made my way back to bed, defeated and feeling the throb of pain in my wrist.

Dan had checked the house over. I had tried to catch the source of the sound. Neither had provided any answers.

Still, the noise was there, and it sounded so much like footsteps I began to wish that I believed in ghosts, just so I could give myself an explanation. Instead, I tried to accept Dan's suggestion: it was the central heating system. The pipes must have pre-existed my parents' residence at Bittersweet, and if Dad had ever had the boiler and system maintained or replaced, I knew nothing about it. Being the middle of winter in a house that would otherwise be too cold to inhabit, I wasn't going to experiment by turning the heating off at night. Ghosts weren't likely to kill me, but hypothermia might.

I was anxious and sleep deprived. That should have been enough explanation, if I could only accept it. Nothing else made sense.

I got back under the duvet, curled my body around Dan's and waited for the drift into darkness.

ELEVEN

From that point on, I had to decide to ignore the padding sound and accept that it couldn't be anything threatening or supernatural. Each night I still heard it. Each morning, I forced myself out of bed, after not having nearly as much sleep as I needed.

By the start of our second working week, I had already learned that I needed to be in the bathroom before Dan got up. For a man, he seemed to have a protracted morning ritual. I had been too late on our second day in the house and had ended up applying my makeup in the car on the way to the station. From that point, as soon as the alarm went off, I kissed Dan and left the bed to make sure I was ready before he needed to perform his routine.

I showered, dressed and plastered foundation and blusher onto my face in the hope that it would make me look slightly less sleep deprived.

Then, down in the kitchen, I made sure that everything was ready for our departure. I plucked our lunchboxes out of the fridge, and set his down on the worktop, ready to go. I couldn't help but think back to how, no matter what was happening, no matter how bad things were between her and Dad, Mum would always make sure my lunch was packed: two finger sandwiches, fruit and a Penguin biscuit – sometimes a Kit-Kat if she'd been shopping; Dad used to eat them before I had a chance to take them to school, so it was pot luck if there was one left for me.

I daydreamed my way through the prep, right up to the point at which I was lifting my own plastic container – filled with leftovers then, rather than the tiny picnic of my childhood – and I'd almost dropped it into my bag before I realised that there was something not quite right. It was too light. Not the kind of tub that felt like it had a slab of last night's lasagne and a dried up (but still delicious on the second day) chunk of garlic bread inside. Gently, I shook the box, trying to feel out the slumping shift of the food inside.

I knew before I peeled the lid back what I was going to find: it was empty. Not empty in a you-never-put-anything-in-here kind of way, but empty in an orange residue on the sides of the tub way. There were a few small pieces of minced beef clinging onto the smears of tomato sauce, giving it an almost visceral effect.

"What the…"

Dan was whistling in the living room by then. I thought it was some old Radiohead song, but I couldn't place it. He was tuneless, but he loved to try. I imagined it was one of the things that could lead us to a divorce court later down the line. Unreasonable differences, your honour. The man can't hold a note.

That was nothing compared to him eating my lunch.

I thought back to the evening before. We had eaten the fresh-from-the-packet meal, not home cooked, because who has time for that when they're working full time and trying to face up to their childhood trauma? I had planned ahead though, getting the family-sized lasagne so we could stretch it to the following day's lunch too. 'Serves six' meant 'serves two plus leftovers'.

If you think it sounds trivial, you've never been sleep deprived, stressed, and scared.

I stared down at the scrapings in the tub and then stepped into the doorway to confront Dan.

"My lunch," I said, trying to keep calm. I cleared my throat and started again. "Dan. Have you any idea what happened to my lunch?" It felt like a rhetorical question when I asked it, because of course he knew. Or course he had taken it.

"You probably ate it," he said, without missing a beat. He didn't even stand still to talk to me, instead blustering out of the room and onto the staircase.

"Dan!" The indignation in my voice slipped out in a whiny squeak. I hated the sound of it.

I ran, yes literally ran, to the doorway and watched as he moved upwards. Something about it infuriated me. He had taken my lunch and couldn't even own up to what he had done. As earth-shattering betrayals go, it wasn't up there with sleeping with my best friend (one reason I avoided close friendships) or emptying my bank account, but in the moment it felt close.

"Dan!" I called, more calmly, but still unable to conceal the irritation I felt.

He stopped, three quarters of the way up, and bent, peering through the bannisters to look at me. It made him appear like he was behind bars. Definitely too strict a punishment for eating my lunch, but only just.

"If you were hungry last night, there were plenty of other things you could have eaten." If I wasn't careful, I was at risk of bursting into tears, and crying over my lost lunch was not likely to be a good look.

"Sure," Dan said. He stood again, moving from the gap in the stairs momentarily, before once more ducking to face me. "Look El, I didn't eat your lunch, okay?" He paused again and then said. "You probably ate it yourself when you were up in the night."

As far as I was aware, I had spent my usual hour or so listening to the padding noise on the landing, trying to remind myself that there was nobody out there, and enviously watching Dan sleep beside me before finally drifting off myself. I'd gone to the bathroom before bed, as I always did, as I always had. That was my routine, and I wasn't old enough to be an up three times in the night kind of woman yet. Besides, for all

I said about knowing there was no one else in the house, there was no way that I was going out there in the dark in the middle of the night on my own.

"What?" I asked, too quietly. Dan had moved on up the stairs, and I could hear him on the landing above.

Pad, pad, pad.

The now familiar sound sent a chill through my already on-edge nerves.

Dan's steps made a heavier thud, though: more of a *pud, pud, pud.*

Probably the extra weight of my lunch, I thought.

I couldn't let it lie.

I flicked my eyes briefly back towards the clock on the kitchen wall. Ten minutes until we had to leave: plenty of time to have it out with him.

I'd never had the joy or misery of siblings, so I'd never had to share anything as a child. What few things were mine were mine. Not that I saw Dan in any kind of messed up way like that, but somehow my personal laws of possession adhered to those rules that I had grown up with.

To some extent, it *was* trivial. If he had asked me, I would have knocked up a sandwich for my lunch and given him the leftover dinner happily. I wanted to please him. Only a few months into our relationship, and with the self-awareness to know that I was letting him see me at my worst, moving back to Bittersweet and picking at the scabs of my life, I wanted to do everything I could to please him.

Still, my legs were taking me through the hallway, up the stairs, and into the bathroom, where he was standing at the sink, toothbrush in his mouth.

"I would have given it to you," I said, now unable to control the tears. I was angry at myself for letting him see my cry like that, and for making a mess of the makeup that I had already spent fifteen minutes applying. I dabbed at my eyes, trying to stop the mascara running down my cheeks, trying to control the damage.

"Oh Ella. Please don't. Not now, okay?" He paused the brushing, but the toothpaste and saliva in his mouth garbled his words.

"I planned our lunches, Dan. I sorted everything out before I went to bed so both of us would have food today. You could have eaten yours. You could have eaten something else. I'm doing my best, okay? Even though I'm having a really, really hard time, I'm doing my best, and this…"

I was in floods of tears by then, and no amount of wiping beneath my eyes was going to stem the flow.

Dan spat a foamy mouthful into the sink and span around to me.

I jerked backwards in a reflex response, almost ducking to avoid a blow, but it didn't come. He shook his head, reached his arms out, and wrapped them around me. I tried to resist as he pressed my head into his chest, both because I was still hyped-up angry at him, and also because I knew there was a good chance that my makeup was going to end up all over his fresh white shirt.

"It's okay," he said. "Come on."

It wasn't okay. I was starting to think that nothing was okay.

"If you took it…" I snorted through the tears.

"Shh," he said, softly. "Shh. Let it go, okay? Let it go."

"Just…" I couldn't give up.

"Shh, Ella. Everything is going to be all right. Everything is going to be all right."

I let the tears flow because that release felt so good. It was almost like the rush of an orgasm after a long dry spell, letting go of something that had been built up inside me.

My lunch was gone. It wasn't coming back. Was there any point in arguing with Dan about it? Was that really going to get me anywhere?

Taking my lunch was a dick move, but I decided that conflict with him was pointless. I was still exhausted, still over-emotional, and the last thing I needed was another row. We both had to go to work. I didn't have the time or the energy to make an even bigger deal of what he had done.

"I guess I get to go to Starbucks today," I said, forcing a smile.

"That's my girl," Dan said, and those words made that smile widen.

At the end of the day, it was lasagne, not the end of the world. I was going to have to make some compromises if I wanted Dan to stick around.

I was his girl, and I wanted it to stay that way.

Some things were worth fighting over, and some were not.

TWELVE

I resolved not to mention the lunch incident again. The thought of him lying to me niggled away, though. I could see it as a symptom of the kind of person he might turn out to be – if you can lie about a portion of pasta, you can lie about anything – but that seemed overly dramatic, and I was already in line for an award in that department.

Being back at Bittersweet was not, in any way, having a positive effect on me. Or on us as a couple. I had to give him some leeway, because I knew for certain that he was making allowances for me.

How little I really knew.

In the office, I tried to think of a way to make things better between Dan and me. I had a lot of thinking time. My work assignment was fine, but just fine. The people in the office all knew each other and had been working together for long enough that I felt like an outsider, excluded from their in-jokes and cosy break time chats. In reality, it suited me fine. The trainers and back room staff mingled and laughed around me. I got on with my job and kept myself to myself.

When I walked down to the coffee shop alone at lunchtime, I stopped in at the food hall and picked up a couple of pizzas and a half-decent bottle of wine. Back in my bedsit, where we had no sofa, but at least you could get a takeaway driver to deliver, we had a habit of crawling into my bed, sharing a meat feast and a Hawaiian, and binge-watching television streams. Now we had a wide-screen, actual furniture, and nowhere to order pizza from. I missed our cramped existence.

In the evening, I tried to be more positive. I heated dinner, poured the wine, and sat snuggled up to him on the sofa, laughing at repeats of Friends. Somehow, I felt ten years younger, the stresses of moving to Bittersweet melting into a warm buzz of togetherness with Dan. Wasn't that why we were there? To be together? To make Bittersweet somewhere that I could call home and feel happy about doing so?

When we had eaten all we could and picked away at the topping from the leftover triangles, Dan pulled me in towards him and kissed me. He tasted of tomato and garlic, and it was enough to send me back to that happy place again, that past that I hadn't appreciated while we were living in it. I hadn't felt the slightest trace of a sexual impulse since we moved into Bittersweet – the tension and traumatic memories put paid to that – but as he moved his hands over me, finally I relaxed into his touch.

I am always careful with alcohol, and I know that there's a slippery path that I can easily stumble upon, but I don't abstain. I like to think I have enough self-control to enjoy a glass or two, and that evening, I believe it helped.

His mouth explored mine, and I responded, unbuttoning his shirt, touching him in a way that the week at Bittersweet had made me forget.

He stood, offered his hand to pull me to my feet, and led me up the stairs.

Everything was perfect until we reached the bedroom.

I don't know how I had expected to feel, sharing the bed that my parents had slept in for more than just sleep. Our own feet made the *pad, pad, pad* sound across the landing, the eager anticipation speeding up that familiar rhythm. As Dan opened the door, though, my heart turned to stone. The tingle that had been running through my body turned to a chill. I looked at the bed in front of us – my parents' bed – and I couldn't go any further.

"What is it?" Dan asked, before I'd even opened my mouth to speak.

Still looking at the bed, I shook my head.

"I can't," I said. My voice was shaking.

He must have been able to tell that I wasn't comfortable, but he let out a sharp laugh.

"What?" he said, near incredulous. "Come on, El."

He reached around me, taking me into an embrace that only made me feel trapped.

I shrugged him off.

"No, Dan. I can't."

The closeness that we had been sharing less than a few minutes before was gone. My skin bristled at his touch, and I wanted to be out of there. Out of that room. Out of that house.

It wasn't my house; it was Dad's.

It wasn't my bed.

There was no way I could let Dan undress me, lay me down there, and do the things I knew he wanted to do. The things I had wanted too until we had walked into that room.

"I'm sorry," I sobbed.

He put the palm of his hand flat on my back. The warmth buzzed through me, and the aroused part of me wanted to snap around, let him grab me and follow through with what our bodies had promised each other. My mind, though, my mind was elsewhere.

"We live here now, Ella. This is our home. This is where we live, and this is where we…"

I knew he was going to use the word for it that I didn't want to hear, so I cut in.

"I know, Dan. I'm sorry. I'm not ready yet, that's all."

I sounded like a virgin, putting off her over amorous partner, and that just wasn't me. It was the truth, though; I couldn't do it.

"Yet?" he said. "You're not ready yet? Do you think you could have let me know that before we started all that foreplay downstairs? It's called foreplay for a reason – because it comes before something."

He's just worked up, I told myself. I couldn't let myself be annoyed with his response, because he was right. This wasn't how normal relationships worked. I was in the wrong, and I knew it.

"Dan, I'm sorry," I repeated. I didn't know what else to say.

The bed stretched out before me, and rather than feeling any kind of passion, when I looked at it, I was repulsed.

He grabbed hold of my shoulders and pulled me to face him. His dilated pupils made his blue eyes appear black, like he wasn't himself anymore.

"I don't like these games, El," he said.

I could feel myself trembling. I trusted him. I didn't think he would do anything to hurt me, but what did I know then? How well did I really know him?

A sickening thought ran through my mind that I had got him worked up, and I should do something about it. That I owed it to him to follow through. I pushed the idea back down into the pit of my traumatised mind. That wasn't how positive relationships worked. That wasn't going to happen in this one.

Instead, I steeled myself and reached out to him, placing a quivering hand onto his chest, just above his heart.

"You've been so wonderful," I shivered. "So patient with me. Please. Just a little longer. I'm sorry about tonight, and believe me, when we were downstairs, I wanted it too. I really did. But…" I gestured around us. "I need time to get used to this. Please."

I saw him gulp, as though he too was adjusting his mindset, levelling himself out. Both of us had got carried away in more ways than one.

"Shit, I'm sorry," he said, wrapping his arms around me. "I'm sorry."

I softened into his embrace, and I knew this physical closeness was opening myself up to an emotional closeness, too. We needed it. We needed that moment. In the confusion of moving to Bittersweet and the mind tricks it was playing on me, the difficulty I was having adjusting to my return, we needed it.

I needed it.

"It won't always be like this." He spoke the words into my hair as he held me to him.

Then, the words were reassuring. I thought there was promise of a happy future in that sentence, but I was wrong.

Instead of getting better, things were about to get worse.

Much worse.

THIRTEEN

When I woke the following morning, I shuffled across to kiss Dan. In his sleep, he withdrew from me, pulling the cover up around his head like a shield against my affection. I almost whined his name, indignant at his rejection, but instead, I let him continue his doze. I didn't need another argument, especially not at half past seven on four hours of sleep.

I was groggy, just as I had been every morning since we moved into Bittersweet. The walk to the bathroom seemed more difficult each day. I swayed against the wall in an almost hangover-like stumble as I made my way along the landing and gave myself a moment to steady myself before carrying on.

I made it to the sink and when I looked into the mirror I saw a pale, drawn face looking back. I'd tied my curls back into a messy knot before bed, and wisps fell around the side of my face. My eyes were bloodshot, my skin so lacklustre that I immediately ran the tap and splashed cold water over my cheeks.

It's a wonder Dan still wants you at all.

My inner voice was unkind, but the thought was not unfounded. I was a mess. Lack of sleep; that's all it was. It would get better; I was sure it would get better.

I applied the mask of make-up, giving colour to my grey complexion, and trying to erase my sunken appearance. Being back at Bittersweet was taking a toll on me in more ways that I could have imagined.

'Doing this for my mum' was beginning to feel like it had never been enough of a reason to return. Was I really that vulnerable that I had jumped at the merest suggestion from a man I hardly knew that coming back to Bittersweet could be a good thing? There were barely any traces of her here. Dad had lived alone in the house without either of us for a decade, and everywhere was imbued with him, and only him. He had thrown away almost everything she ever owned, and the room that had once been mine was empty of everything but furniture. I could sit on the bed that I had slept in as a child, but without my belongings, it felt like a pale replica, no memories attached.

I walked past the door to my former room and turned the handle. I'd barely been inside since I came back. There was nothing to see, so what point was there in revisiting? I'd have it redecorated, turn it into a guest room for guests that I never expected to have. I had no family to visit us, and Dan never talked about his.

When I lived here, there were posters on the wall, the teen bands and actors that took the place of real friends. Now, all I saw were blank spaces, and the window, with its voile veil and barred backdrop. There was nothing left of Mum, and there was nothing left of me.

Starting the day in that introspective fog made me wish for the days when I could warm my cold thoughts with vodka. I had to find something else to bolster myself and lift me out of the funk. I had to look for a reason to carry on, a sign that I was doing the right thing, being there.

I closed the door and skulked down the stairs into the cold downstairs hallway. The heating hadn't kicked in, even though it was programmed to warm the house half an hour before my alarm went off. The wooden boards sent icy jolts through my feet, making me quicken my pace.

I jiggled the thermostat and tried to get the heating to boot up, but it stubbornly refused. I left it alone; it sounded like a Dan problem. I didn't have to resort to Google searches now that I had him.

In the kitchen, I flicked the switch on the kettle, and half expected that to let me down too. It didn't. The red light glowed, and the sound of slowly heating water began. If I couldn't have vodka – and technically I could if I wanted, but I wasn't going to, I really wasn't – I would have strong coffee. No one judges you for a caffeine addiction.

When I reached into the cupboard to pull out a mug, I got the sign that I had been looking for.

I wasn't focusing, mostly due to being too tired, too cold, and generally feeling like crap. My hand fumbled through the assorted cups, and I plonked the random mug onto the work surface. I stretched my arms above my head, shook out some of the tension, linking them behind my back and pushing away from myself like a warmup for exercise that I had no intention of taking. My thoughts swam from Dan and my inability to be a decent girlfriend to the lack of heat in the house, and then on to the general daily ruminations about why I was there and what I really hoped to achieve.

The click of the kettle snapped me back to the present moment, and I plucked a spoon from the drawer, heaped it with coffee, and stopped, spoon mid-air, when I saw the mug.

It was the one that Mum always used. Ugly as hell, white with a faded floral pattern, and that one word, chipped and scratched away from years of use and washing – Mum. I hadn't given her many presents over the years, being a child, and not having any income of my own to buy extravagant gifts.

Dad was against giving me pocket money, so I never had any cash of my own. What I did have was money to buy snacks at school. I had the packed lunches that Mum made me, and she always slipped in that chocolatey bonus, so I decided I would go without the extra treats at break time. I didn't need them, and, as I didn't have any friends, I figured I didn't need to buy anything just because the other kids were.

No one was going to say anything about my lack of strawberry laces or salt and vinegar crisps. It wasn't a lot, but I saved that money, and I bought that mug for her.

She realised what I had done, of course, and I thought at the time that made her love it even more. She knew I had sacrificed for her – albeit in a very small way. But that's what we did for each other. She was my mum; that's what we did.

With my free hand, I reached out and traced my fingers over the letters on the mug. I wasn't ready for the outpouring of emotion that followed. My other hand dropped the coffee laden spoon onto the counter, and I had to steady myself to stop myself slipping to the floor.

Mum and me: a pair against the world. A pair against him. When she was gone, what hope did I have here? Bittersweet was always his; it was never ours. Now it could be. At last, it could be.

FOURTEEN

I was in a daze as I grabbed some kitchen towel and wiped up the coffee granules from the work surface. I'd asked for a sign, and I got one. Maybe Bittersweet did have some sweetness to it after all. Everything had seemed so bleak since I got there, only a few days ago. I couldn't remember having a single positive thought about the place, but finding the mug had given me something to cling to.

She would have thought I was insane, going back there, but she would have understood why. I knew she would have been cheering me on, wherever she was, just like she always did.

But she was nowhere. She was gone. All that was left of her was that mug. And me.

I put Mum's cup back, tucking it behind the others for safekeeping, and pulled out another for my coffee. This time I managed to get the granules, water and a splash of milk together, and I stood against the counter, sipping at the hot coffee. The warmth was so welcome against the chill of the morning. The central heating might not have been working, but the coffee rushed through me, warming me from the inside.

When I'd thought about Dan and I moving in together, I pictured the two of us taking turns to be up first in the morning, each bringing the other coffee and toast in bed, like some fantastical version of a relationship that I'd never experienced but hoped existed. I didn't know then how useless he was in the morning or that he didn't drink coffee or tea. I knew so little about him, but there we were, living as a couple, trying to make something of our thrown together life.

I finished my coffee and sighed into the morning routine. Again, as I did every morning, I took our lunch boxes from the fridge. Tuna sandwiches that day, just the way Mum used to make them, with a smear of pesto on one of the slices of bread. I'd introduced Dan to the idea without telling him where it came from. Not that I wanted to take the credit, but more that sometimes, I just wasn't up to talking about Mum. Not about what happened, and not even about those happy little memories that could still somehow trigger a downward spiral into introspection and thoughts of what I had lost, lost, lost.

I snapped myself out of it before I started to sink. I had found the mug, and that was a sign. It was a positive sign. I couldn't let myself slide down into negative nostalgia again.

Focus, I told myself, as I set his box on the work surface and went to slip mine into my bag.

As I tilted the box to fit, I felt the contents shift.

After the whole missing lasagne incident, I was sure that Dan wouldn't have been enough of a dick to take my lunch again. It seemed like such a minor thing, but at the same time, it was everything. I've always been good at blowing things out of all proportion, but this was a principle. You have your lunch; I have mine. You have your belongings; I have mine. I never had much, but I was fiercely protective of the little I had. Dan was crossing a line that I was prepared to fight to push him back over.

Before I had even opened the box to check, I knew that something was wrong. I was already judging him, my mind spinning through the sentences that I was going to spit at him.

The lunchbox wasn't empty. It was worse than that.

Half of the tuna sandwich was missing.

Folded on top of the remainder was a note.

It looked like a scrap of lined paper that had been torn from a notebook. The jagged edge along the bottom was a giveaway. I could make out a greasy smear and imagined in that moment Dan's mayonnaise covered fingers folding the note and placing it on top of the part of my lunch he had so graciously left for me.

I swore beneath my breath and grabbed the piece of paper. A single word was scrawled across it:

Mine.

What the hell was that supposed to mean? It wasn't *his* lunch.

An overwhelming sense of injustice and downright fury slammed into my chest.

Not again. He couldn't do this to me again.

And leave a note?

Was he playing some kind of game with me? Trying to push the boundaries of our relationship to see how far he could go? I didn't know much about being part of a couple – to be honest, I knew next to nothing – but I knew that what he was doing was wrong. I had seen the way Dad treated Mum, but I'd never stuck around with anyone to see if they would treat me that way before. These power games couldn't be part of a normal, healthy relationship, could they?

If they were, I didn't want it.

It had to stop.

FIFTEEN

I stuffed the note into my pocket and flew upstairs, my *pad, pad, pad* racing across the landing.

Dan was still in the bedroom, but he was at least awake. Half dressed, pulling his sweater over his head, I paused until I could see his face before launching into my attack.

"How could you do this again? What the hell is wrong with you?" I couldn't hold back. "We live together now, and you've got to start respecting me."

Dan stared at me impassively and let me carry on.

"Aren't you going to say something? Can't you apologise? This is messed up, Dan. This is so messed up."

When he rolled his eyes, it was the last straw. I snapped and flew at him. My fists were up, but I had no intention of hitting him. I'd never hit anyone, so where the reflex action came from, I had no idea. Still, I sprang towards him, fuelled by anger and the frustration of his reticence to respond.

Dan reached out and grabbed my wrists, circling one hand around each like hand cuffs, restraining me and stopping me in my tracks.

"Calm down, little girl," he said.

"I'm not a little girl," I spat, "and I won't calm down."

"Someone's going to get hurt if you carry on like this, and it's probably going to be you."

I froze, fists still raised, still in his grasp.

In a mouselike voice that I barely recognised, I asked, "Are you threatening me?"

"Ella," he said. "Come on. Just calm down, okay?"

If he had meant it as a threat, he seemed to reconsider his words, and his tone settled.

"I've just woken up, and you're coming at me with this… whatever it is…"

"You've been awake long enough to eat my sodding lunch again," I said, unable to hold back the venom, but dropping my hands as he tentatively let go of them.

"This again?" He sighed as though he was bored with the conversation already, which needled me even further.

"This again," I said. "I thought I told you…"

He reached forward and placed a finger on my lips. "Stop, El."

Everything he was doing to try to calm me was having the opposite effect.

I ripped his hand away and almost yelled, "You left a bloody note!"

"You're being ridiculous. I don't know what all this is about, but I don't like it, El."

"You don't *like* it? *You* don't like it?" I repeated his words back to Dan, stressing the emphasis. How was this about him and what he liked?

To me, the situation was clear-cut. He had taken my lunch again, not all of it, granted, but that was a minor detail. He had done it again, despite my tears and his reassurances the last time. I was bursting with emotion and starting to feel as though he was part of my problem with Bittersweet, rather than being on my side.

I tugged the note out of my pyjama pocket and rammed it into his face.

"It's your lunch, is it? How the…"

He gave the note a cursory glance before thrusting it back at me.

"I didn't write that, El."

"Oh, shut up," I snapped. "There are two people in this house. We've established that."

"Then there's only one answer, isn't there?"

"That you wrote it."

"That *you* wrote it, Ella."

I actually laughed. One quick, derisive bark.

"I can't even... I don't know what to say to you, Dan. That's just..." I stood, staring at him, turning to the note in my hand, then back to him.

He reached forward and tried to put his hand on my cheek. I yanked my head away.

"Not this time," I said. "You can't just give me all those words and... and..." I stammered, not knowing what to say next.

"What do you want, then?" His expression switched from caring to aggravated. "I don't know what you want from me."

"I want you to respect me, and respect my lunch."

"You sound ridiculous, Ella. Respect your lunch? What does that even mean? And this?" He batted the note out of my hand onto the bedroom floor. "Let me get something clear. I. Did. Not. Write. That. Note."

With each word, he moved closer to me, so that I had to lean back on my heels, and by the end of his sentence, stumbled backwards against the wall.

An echo chill ran through me. A memory of my dad, spitting his words like this. Looming, just as Dan was.

I couldn't let myself cry. Not in front of him. I didn't want him to know that whatever he was trying to do, it was working.

There was a fracture in our relationship, and I didn't know what to do. All I knew was that if it kept widening, I was in danger of falling deep, deep into that chasm between us. That could only lead to pain.

We stood there, our faces inches apart, staring at each other, wordless. My rapid breaths were coming out in tiny white clouds in the house's chill. Dan was more in control of himself. I could tell that his pulse wasn't pounding like the skittering of my scared sparrow heart.

He was in control, but he was not calm. Anything else that I said was bound to lead to an explosion. It was barely eight in the morning, and I had already been through enough of an emotional rollercoaster to send me back to bed. My head was heavy, buzzing with so many emotions that I didn't know what to feel.

Dan took a slight step back, ceding space to me.

"Come on," he said. "Let's go to work and we can talk about everything later."

I knew he was trying to defuse the situation, but it had gone too far for me. I was at breaking point. I shook my head.

"I can't," I said. I kept my voice quiet, hoping that it would at least sound calm. "I think I'm going to phone in sick today."

Dan just nodded. "Sure. Whatever." He stepped around me, heading for the door, and I stood where I was, staring at the empty space where he had been.

Before he left the room, he spoke again, from behind me.

"I know how hard things are, El, but I'm on your side. I'm trying to help you, but you are making it so, so difficult for me."

I heard him, and I wanted to believe him, but my eyes had fallen onto the word written on the note at my feet.

Mine.

The word was nothing, but, at the same time, it was everything. If he was truly on my side, why would he play these games with me, knowing the state I was already in?

When I didn't reply, Dan let out an agitated, exaggerated sigh and walked out of the room. He didn't storm out. He didn't slam the door. He just walked away.

I listened for the sound of his feet on the stairs, the clattering in the kitchen, and it was only when, without either of us speaking another word to each other, he left the house, that I finally let myself cry.

SIXTEEN

If I had thought ahead, and if we hadn't had another of our rows, I would have asked him to take a look at the central heating before he left. I tucked myself back into bed after I heard his car bumping down the field and managed to catch up on some much-needed sleep. When I woke just after noon, my left leg had freed itself from beneath the covers and had an icy pale blue sheen. How I'd slept while one of my limbs was freezing, I have no idea beyond the fact that my body was desperate for rest.

I thought it was Bittersweet that was stopping me from sleeping, but waking up cold yet refreshed, I questioned whether it was actually Dan. Was being with him the reason that I couldn't sleep? Was it that I was constantly stressed and unable to focus? Not having lived with a man before, and then moving in with him was bound to have an effect on my psyche, no matter where we lived. Moving to Bittersweet might just have compounded the stress on my fragile little mind.

Dan was never meant to be my life partner. I had a placement in his office, only three days, but that was enough for us to start talking and arrange to go out for drinks. I didn't have any rules about mixing business and pleasure because where else was I going to meet anyone other than at work? I moved from post to post swiftly enough for it never to cause a problem, anyway. It wasn't like I could have an awkward office environment with someone that I'd been out with when I wasn't sticking around.

Agency work suited me on so many levels.

I'd already left that placement before we had our date. Three days of text flirting was enough build-up for us to hit it off and end up back at my place at the end of the night. Again, I figured I wasn't going to see him again, so what did it matter what a pokey little craphole I lived in?

Of course, I saw him again. And again. He didn't seem to mind that my bedsit was a mess, or that I was. I had no idea how to behave, dating someone. I'd forget to return his calls, leave his messages on read. Looking back, he probably thought I was playing hard to get, or at least that I was playing it cool. Apparently, though, the kind of woman that's not always chasing after you, asking when the next date is going to be, or asking for commitment is exactly what some men are looking for.

I wasn't trying to pin him down because, due to my lack of experience, combined with my almost non-existent self-worth, I didn't even have that on my radar. I was happy in our dating/not dating state. There was finally a man that I wanted to spend time with that actually wanted to spend time with me too. That was enough.

Had we ruined everything by taking the next step, moving to Bittersweet as a couple, and trying to grab more than we needed to be happy together?

Or maybe that is just what people do. Relationships develop. We go from casual to committed and, of course, things change as a result.

I didn't like the changes in Dan, though, not one bit.

The events of the morning were heavy on my mind as I finally pulled myself out of bed and made it back downstairs. The house felt even colder than it had when I had first got up. The day outside was grey and not doing anything to add any warmth to Bittersweet.

Again, I twisted the dial on the thermostat, and again, nothing happened. No click, nothing. I knew where the boiler was, but I didn't have the first idea of what to do with it. Now I was with Dan, I resented being the one to work out how to fix it. He would know, for sure. I decided to hack it out and leave it to him when he got home. It was the least he could do, all things considered. I had blankets and jumpers, and the experience of living for eighteen years in that bleak house on the edge of the moors. One bitter day wasn't going to defeat me.

My work placement had been understanding about my day off, considering I was only there to stand in for someone else who was on long-term sick leave. Calling in was something I was usually reluctant to do; if I flipped off too many days, I was less likely to get chosen for future jobs. My non-career career suited me perfectly, and I didn't want to mess it up. Even after taking the morning in bed, though, I felt dog rough. It was almost like a hangover, that leaden headedness and the drudgery of movement I felt when I dragged myself through the hallway.

I shuffled into the kitchen, convinced that coffee and toast were the pick-me-ups I needed. I couldn't face the gammy softness of tuna mayo, and eating that half sandwich would have raised my hackles again. Toast, maybe jam. That was the cure for all evils.

The bread was in one of those dated pine boxes with the sliding hatch. I was fascinated by it as a kid, but seeing it with my fresh adult eyes, it seemed unhygienic and took up too much room on the work surface. My sluggish mind was so caught up in these thoughts that I almost missed it.

Almost.

On the kitchen counter was a note, scrawled in the same spidery handwriting that I had seen in my lunchbox.

Don't blame him.

Instinctively, I span around, looking to see if there was someone there, watching me. An unknown that had taken to sneaking into my kitchen – our kitchen – just to leave stupid notes and generally antagonise me.

"What the hell?" I muttered out loud.

Don't *blame* him?

Of course, I guessed that the '*him*' in question was Dan. Nothing else made sense. Why Dan would leave me a note referring to himself in third person didn't make sense either, but that was the only reasonable assumption I could make.

I wasn't feeling particularly reasonable.

Leaving the note on the counter, without even touching it, I stepped away, as if slapped.

I knew Dan had checked the entire house through, but that was then. Could someone have got in since then? Was I really alone?

Adrenaline thudding, I ran to the front door and tugged at it, testily.

If there was someone else in the house, there was no one that could help me. The nearest houses were too far away to hear any disturbance – or to respond if I yelled for help. My phone was upstairs, next to the bed, where I'd plugged it in the night before. Dad had ditched the landline in the decade that they had gone out of fashion.

As I pulled the door, I muttered a silent plea to the universe.

Don't let it open.

I pulled, and it didn't move.

Such a wave of relief hit me that I collapsed against the wood, pressing my back against the cold surface and sinking down to my haunches on the floor.

Of course, it didn't open.

Dan had locked it on his way out. I thought back to earlier in the morning, listening to the sounds he made as he got ready and left the house. I had heard the jangle as he locked the door. He had locked it; it was locked.

The only explanation then was my first assumption: he had left that note for me. It seemed like a stupid thing to do, considering that he had denied taking my lunch and leaving that first note in place of my half sandwich.

It all sounded so petty when I repeated it in my head, but if the notes weren't enough to piss me off, the principle of what Dan had done was.

Don't blame him?

Dan was messing with me. Of that, I was becoming certain.

But why? What was he trying to do?

SEVENTEEN

The draft blowing beneath the front door forced me back to my feet. If I stayed there, I would freeze. Dan would come home, try to open the door, and wouldn't be able to move it, my corpse acting as the perfect door stop. A fitting end for me, though, pressed up against the exit to that house.

I had to make light of the situation, because if I didn't my over-active imagination would spiral out of control.

The simplest explanation is usually the best explanation. Two people lived at Bittersweet Acres. If I hadn't written the notes, Dan had. Simple.

I wasn't thrilled with that reasoning, but I knew it was the only thing that made sense. The argument, like the heating, could wait until he came home.

I forced myself back to the kitchen, brewed coffee and fed the toaster. Despite not having eaten yet, I begrudgingly ate half of my toast and didn't have the appetite for more. I was starting to get the dark swell of a migraine. It wasn't there yet, but I could sense the first dull waves creeping into my temples.

There was nothing else to do than to take myself through to the living room and curl on the sofa, pulling a thick blanket over me as a barrier to the cold. We were prepared for low temperatures at Bittersweet. It was the last house that walkers passed as they hiked up onto the moors, or, more positively, the first that they came to on their return. Bittersweet bore the brunt of the wind, and when the snow came, which it did most winters, we had found ourselves cut off; isolated. The gritters never bothered to drive up the narrow track that led to our drive. We spent the snow weeks alone; abandoned.

There was no snow then, but there I was, just as alone with only the ghosts of my past and the building agony of my migraine.

By the time I heard Dan's key turn in the lock, my migraine had escalated from a swell to a storm. The outside world was already darkening, but I had left the lights off in the living room. It had been a while since my last attack. Since I left Bittersweet years ago, my headaches had stopped, or at least the ones that hadn't been self-inflicted. Still, I remembered the little things that I could do to mitigate. Darkness, warmth, water and whatever analgesia I could find. Today it had been ibuprofen; it wasn't helping.

When I had found the note, earlier in the day, I had envisaged a confrontation between Dan and me. He would walk through the door, and I would launch my questions at him, not backing down this time, not until he explained exactly what he was up to with the notes.

Now that my brain had become a swirling maelstrom, there was no way that I could do that. I would have had trouble even standing, at that point, never mind running to Dan and yelling out accusations. Even the thought of it made me nauseated.

He flicked the light by the front door on, which cast a dull yellow glow into the living room. I could bear that, but only just. I heard his *pad, pad, pad* along the hall, then he popped his head around the doorway.

"Hey," he said with a smile. "How are you feeling?"

He looked at me, buried beneath the blanket, and then turned his eyes to the ceiling light. Without asking, he switched it on.

The light hit me like jagged shards, piercing my temples, driving into my head.

"Turn it off," I groaned, quietly.

"What?" he squinted his eyes, as though that was going to help him hear me better.

"Turn it off!" I snapped, knowing that raising my voice would cause me even more pain, but that I had to do it anyway.

Dan stared at me and flipped the switch back off.

"Great to see you too," he mumbled, before leaving the room and shuffling down to the kitchen.

I listened to him clatter his lunchbox into the dishwasher and open a cupboard in what I expected was probably a search for snacks. He was whistling to himself again, that same song that I still couldn't work out. Every note made me wince.

I pulled the blanket up over my head, trying to block out the light, the cold, the sound. Dan.

Dan made a big deal of coming back into the living room, picking at a bag of crisps, and plonked himself into the armchair. Even from beneath my hiding place, I could hear the crunching and rustling, and I wanted to scream at him to stop.

He switched on the television, and I pulled back the blanket just enough to be able to see him.

"I have a migraine," I said, keeping my voice as steady and low as possible.

Dan paused, a crisp halfway on its journey to his already open mouth.

Giving me a frown, he took a moment to work out what to say.

"Sorry, love. Can I get you anything?"

He cast his eyes around my immediate area.

"Water? Tablets? Have you taken any?"

"Yeah," I managed to say. "I had some."

"No good?" he asked. As though suddenly gaining awareness, he set his crisp bag down, picked up the remote, and muted the television.

"You should go up to bed," he said. "It'll be quiet up there. I'll put the heating on; it's freezing in here."

I wanted to tell him I couldn't face climbing the stairs, that I didn't want to be in that bed, in that room anyway. If I went up, I would settle in my old room, the one where I had hidden away so many times before. I didn't think I could hide from a migraine, but maybe from what was causing it.

"It's broken," I said, economical with my words, each one more painful to speak.

"Huh?" Dan grunted.

"The heating," I managed to say. Every syllable stabbing another splinter into my tender skull.

He raised his eyebrows in a gesture of understanding.

"Right. Really? Okay."

He picked the bag back up and stuffed another pawful of crisps into his mouth, licking at the salt on his fingers. I wanted to vomit. I could feel it rise in my throat, but I didn't have the energy to move.

I definitely didn't have the energy to talk to him about the note.

Don't blame Dan.

No, that's not what it said, was it?

Don't blame him.

Maybe it didn't mean the lolloping caveman sitting in front of me at all. Maybe it meant Dad.

I'd spent the past week hung up on my memories of how awful things had been here at Bittersweet, growing up. I had been blaming Dad, the ghost of my dad, for everything. Everything that had happened before, and everything that was happening now. For someone who didn't actually believe in ghosts, I was letting supernatural ideas crowd my mind. No wonder I was losing sleep and getting migraines.

"Uh. You okay?" Dan peered at me with a look of concern, sitting forward in his chair, and I realised that I had zoned out for a minute there.

"Just thinking," I said, quietly, almost breathing the sentence.

"I know things are tough, and that you're not feeling great, but, um, you're acting kind of weird."

"I… feel… weird." It was a struggle to get the words out.

He wiped his hands down his sweater, brushing off the remains of crisp crumbs, and crouched over beside me on the floor next to the sofa.

Don't blame Dan, I thought.

I shook my head, and felt my brain thud from side to side, like the half tuna sandwich, given the extra space to move in the box. My thoughts were becoming a soupy muddle.

Don't blame him.

"What?" Dan moved closer to me, turning his ear to my mouth. I had spoken out loud, but not quite loudly enough to hear.

"It's all me," I whispered.

Dan placed a cold, slightly rough hand on my forehead. I flinched, but then relaxed into it, enjoying the chill against the booming pain.

"You're hot. I don't think you're well, El. Let me get you upstairs, and I'll look after you, all right?"

All I ever wanted was for someone to look after me. But not like that. Not like that.

The threat of vomit was still bubbling, and I could barely keep my eyes open against the light, the overstimulation of the outside world. Everything was working against me to make me feel worse.

"I'm going to pick you up and take you to bed, okay? I'll bring you some more painkillers, and you see if you can sleep."

How could I blame Dan? All Dan had ever done was try to look after me.

I let my head move in the slightest nod and didn't fight against him as he slipped his arms beneath me and scooped me up.

One arm under my back, the other supporting my legs, I rested my head onto his chest as he carried me up the stairs. It seemed effortless to him, as though I were a child that had fallen asleep on the sofa that he was placing into bed.

The confrontation that I had envisaged, waving the note at him, getting to the bottom of why he had written it, and what he was trying to do, was forgotten. If I had the strength to talk to him, then, on that evening, things might have worked out differently. There was still time then, to change things, and to avoid what was going to come next.

Once he had laid me down on the bed, though, and left me in that room, my fate was sealed.

EIGHTEEN

When the migraine was still there the following morning, I gave up hope of recovery. I decided to hibernate, hide myself away in the darkness that didn't help my condition, but didn't exacerbate it, either. Even drawing back the curtains, letting the creep of the day into the room caused shard-like stabbing pain that layered upon the already throbbing agony that filled my head.

Just flu, I told myself, as I rubbed my hand along the aching muscles of my legs, taking every ounce of my effort to try to soothe the stiff cramping discomfort. Just flu, and not worth suffering the trek back down to Doctor Wilson's surgery for.

In truth, there was another reason that I didn't want to go back there. Wilson knew everything about me, and he knew everything about my family. He knew what had happened to Mum, and I didn't want him to think that I was going spinning down that same downward spiral she had. Hearing noises, finding notes, and the insane paranoia of suspecting Dan. They all added up to one thing.

I was starting to doubt myself; I didn't need medical confirmation that moving back to Bittersweet had knocked me off balance.

I decided to ride it out. Flu sorted itself out over a few days. I needed to keep hydrated, in a warm, dark place.

Dan wasn't having any of it. He was home from work, like clockwork, at half-past five, and, after clattering in the kitchen for what felt like hours, but was actually only a matter of loud minutes, he came up to our room.

Day one, he had been sympathetic and caring. By day two, it was starting to fade. I was becoming a problem. He stood over me with a look of impatient disappointment.

"You can't lie in bed all day, Ella. Come on. Please."

"I can't get up. My head…"

"Open the window then. Get some fresh air. Or, please, come out for a walk with me."

I pulled the duvet up over my head, cocooning myself away from his whining. Of course, he leaned over and yanked it back down.

"I've got the flu," I moaned. "I need to rest."

Unceremoniously, he reached out and placed his palm against my forehead. I was about to pull back and complain, but the coolness of his touch was as soothing as his callousness was irritating. I let it be.

"You don't have a fever," he said. "Last night you were warm, but today..." He withdrew his hand and shrugged, without finishing his diagnosis.

I didn't trust his medical opinion, but his was the only one I had. I felt hot, but I allowed for the fact that it was down to spending the day in bed under our feather down duvet.

"I ache," I said, as quietly as I could manage. "My head. My arms... legs." I moved my limbs pathetically, like a tiny bird, fallen from the nest trying to prove that there was still some life left in them.

Dan watched me, unsmiling, and said, "I'll run you a bath then. Soak for a while. See if it helps your muscles feel any better, hmm?"

Getting out of bed sounded like a momentous effort, but the thought of lying in the warm water, feeling the relief of it on my skin, was appealing.

I managed a nod and wished I had kept my head still as soon as I moved. I winced and then faked a smile to please him.

"Thanks," I mumbled. How I was going to get there, I didn't know, but I had to move. He was right.

Dan kissed me on the forehead, and I heard his steps padding across the landing into the bathroom.

While Dan was gone, I made small movements, bringing up one limb and then another, trying to stop my body from fighting my commands. *Keep still*, it seemed to tell me with every effort. The slightest shift brought shudders of pain through my body, and my head was heavy with the pounding throb of migraine. The glass of water on the bedside table had been standing all day, but I forced myself to a sitting position, taking my time as much as I could, and took one mouthful. I tugged on the stiff wooden drawer below to grasp a strip of ibuprofen and knocked two back with a second gulp. He would bring me more water now he was home. He would look after me now.

Water. I couldn't hear the filling of the tub, and my heart rate sped up with the fear that he had forgotten me. I didn't want to take that walk to the bathroom, but Dan was home. Dan was caring for me, and I wanted that. Lying here in bed, what was I? A burden, a whiny girl feeling sorry for herself. Jacksons don't do that. A Jackson doesn't let aches and pains stop them. I heard the words in my head in my father's voice and felt a wave of nausea sweep through me. I gulped again, keeping the sips of water and painkillers down.

Dan and Dad were not the same.

And I was not that little girl anymore.

I waited. I listened for the sound of Dan along the corridor. I couldn't have missed the creaking of the stairs if he had gone back down. Each step made the same sound I remembered from when I was a child. I had learned which part of the wood I could stand on in silence, when I didn't want to be heard – which was most of the time.

"Dan?" I couldn't bring myself to shout, through the stabbing pain, but I raised my voice as much as I could.

No reply.

I screwed my eyes tightly shut, clenching against the thunder inside me, and forced my voice louder.

"Dan?"

Nothing.

"Dan?"

I couldn't bear to shout again.

I reached over to the bedside table, picked up the lamp, and tapped it against the surface, making a knocking sound that echoed around the pain chamber of my skull.

That got his attention. I could hear the soft thucking of his footsteps in the hall. He was downstairs, after all. How had I missed it? I heard the rising movement as he came up the stairway, the *pad, pad, pad* on the landing.

He burst through the door.

"What are you doing?" His face contorted with annoyance. "Is this how you summon me now? What the hell is wrong with you?"

"My head," I managed to say. He wasn't exactly shouting, but his voice was too loud. It would have been too loud even without the inconvenience of my migraine, but with it, it was unbearable.

"Yes, yes," he said. "Your head. You have a headache, I get it, but El, I'm not your slave. I've been at work all day while you've been lying here, and to be honest, I just want to chill for a while, okay?"

I tried to nod, but it was too uncomfortable, so I squeaked a low *yes*.

"Call me if you want something. Don't do this." He picked up the lamp and banged it sharply, three times. Each thud sent daggers into my temples.

"I tried to call you. You didn't hear me."

"No. Well, try getting up then. You could open the door, try to do something for yourself." He shook his head as though he couldn't quite believe how lazy I was. "If I'd known this is what you were going to be like…" He didn't finish the sentence.

I wanted to ask, "What? What if you knew I was like this?" But then a second thought entered my mind – what was I like? What was wrong with feeling ill and needing something from your partner? The truth was, I didn't know. I had never seen what happened when someone cared about someone enough to look after them in their time of need.

Instead of questioning, I lifted my eyes and said, "Sorry."

Had he forgotten about the bath he said he would run for me? It seemed unlikely; it had been his idea, after all. Yet here he was, short on patience and on the defensive.

Dan let out a long sigh, running his fingers through his thick dark hair, and then flopped to sit on the bed by my side.

"Look, I'm sorry, Ella. Work is really tough this week. The commute is harder than I thought. I'm trying to adapt to living here with you. You're... well, this is much more of a challenge than I expected, okay? We've been here for how long? A week? You're hearing noises, crying all the time. You're up half the night, and then wondering why you're having these headaches. And all that crap with your lunches and stupid notes?" He was shaking his head, as though he had no idea how he could cope with an inconvenience like me.

Everything he said was true. I'd not exactly been a bundle of joy to live with.

He turned slightly, so we were directly face-to-face with each other, and cleared his throat before speaking again.

"I have to ask, Ella. Do you think this house is haunted? Is that what's going on here?"

"What? Uh, no!" My indignation made me choke out the words too loudly, and they stung. "No, I told you," I said more quietly. "I don't believe in ghosts. Not the kind you mean, anyway."

"Then what kind? What are you talking about?"

"I think you can be haunted without ghosts being real. Ghosts haunt minds, not places. My dad, my mum even, everything that has happened to me in this house. Those are the ghosts. They are what haunt me. I can't move away from them. I can't move forwards. I thought I could do this, but look at me. Look what's happening to me."

He reached towards me and stroked my hair.

"Ella. This is all in your head, okay? If you can understand that, perhaps you can start to, I don't know, deal better with being here. Everything that's happening, you're doing it to yourself. I'm here for you, but I think only you can stop this."

I was too tired to fight, and my thoughts were clouded by my migraine. I should have stopped then, thought about what he had said, and asked questions.

Instead, I leaned into him and let him take me in his arms. All I wanted was for everything to be okay. I wanted a happy life with a caring partner; I wanted the life that my mum had never found here. If I was doing this for her, I had to stop treading the same path that she had. If I let myself repeat her mistakes, I was going to end up losing my mind in exactly the same way.

"I know it's my fault," I said, and words *don't blame him* echoed through the cotton wool fuzz of my mind.

Don't blame him.

I could only blame myself.

NINETEEN

I slept through to the following morning, and when I awoke, there was no sign of Dan. I hadn't plugged my phone in to charge the night before, so I had no idea of the time. I reached a sleepy arm over to connect the phone to its charger and flopped back against the pillow.

The soaring pain in my head hadn't left. Or perhaps it had left and returned. I had slept, after all. I had slept through the night for the first time since I'd been back at Bittersweet Acres. Despite the agony of my migraine, I couldn't help but be grateful for the rest.

A thought twisted its way into my aching mind: had Dan given me something to make me sleep? I had a vague, cloudy memory of him leaning me forward, putting two pills into my hand, lifting a glass of water to my lips so I could sip and swallow. The more I thought about it, the clearer the image became.

Painkillers, I told myself. *Just painkillers.*

I remembered him settling me into bed for the night, and stroking my forehead.

Just painkillers.

I tugged at the drawer beside the bed and stuck my hand inside. I wasn't looking, just reaching, shuffling my fingers around, trying to make contact with what I was searching for. Pens, a notepad, junk.

My grip closed around the small cardboard box, and I pulled it out. Ibuprofen. Four gone from the pack. I'd taken two earlier yesterday, Dan gave me two before bed. Was that right? Of course, they were just painkillers. It wasn't like he was going to have a stash of... what? Sedatives? Rohypnol? What kind of man did I think he was?

I didn't want to think about the answer to that question; I was ashamed of some of the thoughts I had been having about him.

I popped two pills from their bubbles and tipped them into my mouth. There was a full glass of water beside the bed; Dan must have left it for me before he went to work.

If he had spoken to me that morning, I couldn't remember. If I had said anything to him, I hoped it was only positive appreciation.

My phone let out a triple buzz as it kicked into life, greedily sucking at the power that it had managed to drink up. 10:38am. I'd slept since when? 6:30 last night? I ran through what I could remember. He'd come home, we talked, I took a bath, and then…

A message popped up on my screen.

Hope you're feeling better today. Love you.

We had barely said those words to each other, him being too manly, and me being an idiot, but there they were. My breath caught in my throat, and I could feel my eyes beginning to prickle.

Love you.

Even through the agony of my migraine, I smiled.

The phone screen was too bright, though, and I set it back down on the bedside table.

Love you too, I mouthed.

Despite the persistent nausea, I had the vague awareness that I needed to eat. I'd managed toast the day before, I could do it again.

Give it ten minutes for the pills to kick in.

It was a sound idea.

The ibuprofen didn't rid me of the pain, but it made it more manageable. Once I could bear to move, I did so, slowly, slipping my feet to the floor, and standing, carefully, stepping tentatively towards the door.

The house was warmer. Dan must have got the boiler working, because when I hovered my hand over the radiator, I felt the heat rising again.

He was looking after me, just like he'd said.

That note. *Don't blame him.* The words made sense, even if the origin of the note was a mystery.

Not a mystery, I told myself. *Dan.*

Of course, Dan, of course.

If I had been well enough to ask him about it, he would have told me that. It was a little joke, wasn't it? Trying to lighten the mood after the whole eating my lunch incident. And the repeat of that *incident*. Thinking about that brought my face to a frown.

Let it go, I said, repeating the words I'd heard from Dan. When was that? Yesterday? The day before?

Despite the subsiding pain, my head felt as though it had been stuffed with cotton wool. I couldn't grasp onto a clear thought. Everything felt muggy, muddy, muddled.

I made it down the stairs, clinging to the banister as I took each slow step forwards. The wood was cold on my bare feet and I wished I'd had the strength to dress. Reaching the hallway, and the comfort of carpet, was a warm relief. I had slippers by my bed; I wasn't thinking clearly. I wasn't thinking at all.

My balance wasn't quite there, and I made my way along the hall in a boozy swagger, steadying myself with one hand against the wall.

That nefarious thought popped into my head again: *He drugged me.*

"Don't be so…" I started the sentence out loud, and both my words and my movement forwards jarred to a halt as I saw what was in front of me.

The kitchen door was closed. At eye level – directly at my eye level – was a scrap of paper, held up by a torn piece of sticky tape.

I withdrew the hand that had been steadying my balance, slapping it over my gaping mouth. Still, the sound of my stunned yelp escaped into the empty hallway.

Two words. That same shuddering handwriting.

Get out.

TWENTY

The last thing I remember was the door slipping away from me, the room spinning, and the merciful cushioning of the carpet as I fell to the floor. My head thucked against the wall, and blackness took me.

When the room swam back into focus, I wasn't sure whether the pain was from my returning migraine or from my head's contact with the papered brickwork. All I knew was that the intense throbbing was back. How long had I been down? I couldn't check the time; my phone was still upstairs. The nearest clock was in the kitchen with its ominous warning note telling me to keep out. No. Get out.

Get out.

It took my eyes twenty seconds to focus. The blur of pain and the confusion of waking on the hallway floor slowed down the signals to my brain. Everything shimmered in front of me like a mirage in the vastness of a desert.

The thought made me shiver, and then I realised it wasn't the thought having that effect at all, it was the cold. At some point between the time I got out of bed, stuttered downstairs and found myself in front of yet another weird note, the heating had decided to quit on me again.

It seemed I couldn't rely on anything anymore. Not the heating, not myself, and perhaps not Dan.

When my vision cleared, I looked up, above me, to the door, looming over where I was sprawled. The note was still there. I don't know why I had expected otherwise, but part of me hoped I had imagined it, that I was most definitely alone in the house, that Dan wasn't playing this ridiculous game with me, that ghosts definitely were not real and couldn't use a pen even if they were.

How would a ghost tear sticky tape?

I let myself laugh at the ridiculous thought, because really, I didn't know what else to do.

Shit. Get a grip, Ella.

I managed to get to my feet with more effort than the task should have taken. Every movement was sluggish and consumed both my mental and physical energy.

Again, I steadied myself, and stood eye-to-eye with the two words on the paper in front of me.

Get out.

I wanted to come up with a rational explanation for what I was seeing, but I couldn't think through the ripping feeling in my brain.

The handwriting was the same as the two previous notes. They were large, childlike circles of letters, shaky, as though they had been written with the author's non-dominant hand. I stepped back from the door, ripped the note from the sticky tape, and stumbled my way back upstairs.

Where had I put the other notes? My mind's eye pictured them: on the work surface in the kitchen. Dan had probably thrown them away. This one was enough. I'd fish through the trash if I had to, though.

I made it back to the bedroom, knelt down in front of the wardrobe, and tore open the doors. I hadn't taken much with me to Bittersweet, so searching through my possessions for what I was looking for wasn't going to be a hard job.

The box was tucked away at the bottom, behind my shoes. I swiped them out of the way and brought it forward, hastily yanking off the lid before it was even on the floor in front of me. I sat, legs apart, with the box between them and rooted through it, like a sniffer dog, searching for evidence.

Receipts, tickets for gigs I'd been to over the years, a few photographs I'd taken the trouble to have printed. I didn't stop to reflect on any of the memories attached to them as I rifled through the pile. Then I saw what I was looking for. A birthday card.

It felt like forever since Dan and I were sitting in my room, sharing our usual date night pizza on my birthday. He'd been late arriving, and turned up with a supermarket bag-for-life in hand. I had a tiny television that I'd picked up from the second-hand furniture store, and we sat on the bed, watching a crappy rom com I'd chosen for the occasion. I don't even like that kind of film, it just seemed appropriate for my birthday. That's how malleable I am: even when no one can see, I do what's expected of me. No wonder I'm such a mess.

After the pizza, film, and inevitable birthday intercourse, he reached into the bag and pulled out an envelope and a badly wrapped present. The gift was a teddy bear, about the size of a coffee mug, with a squashed face and rainbow coloured panel on its tummy saying "Happy Birthday!". It was the sort of thing I would have bought for a kid, if I knew any. Still, he had made the effort, and I was grateful enough to thank him genuinely.

Sometime between then, only a month before my dad's death, and now, I'd lost the bear, or thrown it away, I couldn't remember. But here, buried with the rest of the memories I'd managed to hold on to, was the card.

I almost ripped it, pulling it from the box and bringing it up so I could read what was written inside. I knew what it said, but that wasn't what I was looking for. It was Dan's writing that I was interested in. Did the writing in the card match the handwriting on the notes? I had to know. It was the only chance I had of proving to myself that he had written them.

I choked back a sob as I held the note against the writing in the card. The hooped vowels and clumsy consonants of *Get out* were nothing like the measured, tidy slant of *Have a perfect birthday*.

No, I barked, shoving the card away from me, back into the box. *No.*

If they had matched, it would have proved something. Now all I had were more questions and more doubts. He could change his handwriting, make me think it wasn't him. The note was written in such a different style that it was almost evidence that it *was* him that had written it. Wouldn't he want to change his writing as much as possible?

I was missing the point, though.

I still couldn't get my head around why he would write notes like those. Okay, he may have wanted to make a joke about my lunch. Not funny, but at least it was an explanation. Then he decided to carry on with it, trying to be endearing, or cute, I didn't know which, with his *don't blame Dan* effort.

Don't blame him. Of course, *don't blame him.*

But this? *Get out?*

I sat, sprawled in front of the box filled with the memories of my past, trying to put the pieces of my present together.

Dan didn't want me to leave Bittersweet. It was him that wanted us to come here. I would have been more than happy to let the place go, sell up and move on with my life. Had I ever moved on, though? I'd said that I was going there for Mum, but I knew deep down that I was returning to - once and for all - try to move on; to overcome the ghosts of my past.

Could they really be trying to overcome me?

TWENTY-ONE

I threw the card back into the box and shoved my collected memories into the bottom of the wardrobe where I had found them.

Checking Dan's handwriting hadn't helped at all.

There was no way that I was going to accept there could be a supernatural explanation for what was happening. That would mean going back on everything I'd ever believed. I wasn't prepared to let go of my rational thoughts just because of some strange noises and ominous notes. The padding sounds were the normal workings of the house, surely. The notes, well, if they weren't written by me, there was only Dan to blame. No matter what the words on paper said.

I perched on the edge of the bed and picked up my phone. The green bar was full; it was fully juiced, so I plucked out the charger and flicked open the screen.

Settling the scrap of paper down on the bed, I held my phone above it and took a photograph of the words. *Get out.* I wasn't going anywhere. Instead, I typed out a sharp message to Dan:

This isn't funny.

I attached the photo and sent both off to him.

To be honest, I didn't know what else to say. Regardless of the lack of evidence from the birthday card, I knew Dan had written the notes, but I realised I didn't want to admit it to myself.

Even though I had never meant to stumble into this long-term relationship with Dan, I liked him from the start. I liked how he made me feel, and I liked how he made me feel about myself. Being with Dan had given me hope I wasn't as messed up as I always assumed. Before him, I'd get imposter syndrome as soon as I started to grow any kind of emotional attachment to anyone. I wasn't good enough, pretty enough, interesting enough. I wasn't enough of anything to be worthy of love.

Sure, you can trace that back to Bittersweet and the kind of upbringing I had, but even though my dad was ice cold to Mum and to me, I had all the love that I needed from her. As I thought of Mum, I subconsciously raised my hand up to the enamel clip in my hair. That piece of her I always carried with me. It had become a symbol to me, over the years, that someone, once, had loved me.

Not enough to stay, though.

I tried to push that thought out of my mind.

How could I understand what Mum had been going through? How could I ever judge her for finding the only way out that she could? Dad pushed and pushed until she was at the edge, with nowhere else to go but down, down, down.

Sitting on the edge of the bed, the bed that had been hers, thinking about how I had lost her, was no good for my already fractious mind, and I knew it.

I took one look at my phone. Dan had seen my message, but he hadn't replied. The photo of the note was on my screen, the scrap of paper beside me on the bed.

The paper.

I span and yanked open the drawer beside the bed. When I had been scrambling for the tablets, I'd felt a notepad in there, hadn't I? I was too focused on getting the painkillers

– and it was about time I had more – that I hadn't stopped to think about the notepad.

My hand landed straight on it, and I plucked it out, throwing it onto the bed. Before looking at it, I treated myself to two more ibuprofen. I couldn't remember when I'd taken the last, but two too many wasn't going to kill me, and my headache felt like it might.

Swallowing, I flipped open the cover of the notebook.

A ball formed in my throat, and my breath stopped midway to my mouth.

The paper was identical to the paper with the two words written on it. Same blue-vein lines, same spacing, and that same cheap-feel thinness. I'd picked this pad up in one of my placements. The cover had the name of the company embossed on it; heavy black letters embedded in the green background. It was designed to look expensive, but it was flimsy and poor-quality inside.

I ran a page between my fingers, making certain that my eyes were not deceiving me. Pad in one hand, note in the other, there was no difference at all.

Squinting at the top blank page, I could just about make out the imprint that had been left when the last words had been written on the previous sheet.

The looping vowels of the note had left their mark on my pad. I ran a finger over the letters.

A ghost of the words remained: *Get out*.

There was no mistaking.

The pad was more evidence, then. If anyone had come into the house to play mind games, they couldn't have come into the bedroom, reached into my drawer and borrowed a sheet of paper without waking me.

Dan, Dan, Dan. It had always been Dan.

I aimed my phone at the notebook, trying to capture the image of the depressed copy left by the pen, but I couldn't quite get it to work. All I got were shots that looked like a blank page; it was useless.

At least I had the notebook. I could confront him as soon as he got home.

He still hadn't replied to my message. The last words I had received from him were '*love you*'. I shook my head and threw my phone across the bed.

This isn't love. This isn't how love works.

I wasn't even sure how it did work, but I knew it didn't involve whatever mind games he was playing. I had the proof, and there was no way he could deny it.

TWENTY-TWO

I'd fully intended to go back downstairs after finding the pad. Instead, I woke up to the sound of Dan's key in the front door and the realisation that I'd slept through the day.

I must have needed it, I thought. There had been so many sleepless nights and so much anxiety since I'd moved back to Bittersweet. My body must have been desperate to catch up; I was happy to let it.

I'd like to say that I felt a weight had been lifted after I found the evidence to confront Dan, but with the pounding pain still knocking me out of shape, and the heart-sink uncertainty about my future if Dan and I were to separate, I couldn't quite find that level of positivity.

Downstairs, I heard Dan moving around, but I stayed beneath the cover, warm, quiet, and safe.

Or so I thought.

Finally, he made his way up to check on me.

"Been in bed all day?" he asked.

I gave him a look that was meant to show him how pissed off I was, and said nothing.

"Not talking to me? Okay." He turned and stepped back onto the landing.

"Yes," I said flatly.

He looked over his shoulder, and waited, as though I ought to say something else. When I didn't, he took another couple of steps towards the top of the stairs. It was another game, but if I wanted to get him into the bedroom and talk to him about the note, the pad, the proof, I would have to play along.

"Dan," I said. "Come back."

I could see from the heave of his shoulders that he was sighing, but I couldn't hear it. He paused for a moment before dropping his hand from the banister and coming back towards me.

"I'm tired, Ella. Do we have to go through all this again?"

No asking me how I was. No mention of the text message I'd sent him, the picture of the note. Nothing.

"I'm tired too," I replied, and even though I had slept for most of the day, I was. My head, aching though it was, also felt cloudy with sleeplessness. It made no sense. All I could think, through that fog of pain and fatigue, was that the migraines were having that effect on me. It was hard to truly relax with that hammer banging away inside my head.

"Okay then," he said, as though we had made an agreement. "How are you feeling? Apart from tired?"

"Pissed off, actually," I said. I pulled myself up to a sitting position and felt around on the bed, trying to find where I'd left the notepad.

This time, when Dan sighed, I couldn't miss it.

"Oh, I'm sorry to inconvenience you, Dan," I spat. "But I feel like crap and the last thing I needed today was another stupid game of following the clues from you."

"Right," he said. "The note." His voice was emotionless and unapologetic. If I had expected more, I would have been disappointed.

"The note." I had to raise my voice, regardless of the pain it caused me. "I'm going through enough, okay? I don't need this."

"Same, Ella. Same."

"Then why are you doing this? Is it meant to be a joke? A game? What?"

His face was stern, and he looked me dead in the eye.

"Please Ella. Stop this."

"Me stop? Me?" I tugged at the notepad and waved it at him. "What's this then? I suppose this was me as well?"

Dan bent closer to look at the blank page, confusion making his eyes narrow.

"Ella, please," he said, looking back at me.

"What is it? Huh? What?"

"It's a notepad, El. I'm not sure what you want me to say."

"Look." I pointed at the page, but as I did so, I realised that there was no indentation, no sign that the pad had been used to write the words on the note at all. My face fell, and he must have noticed.

"El. This is all in your mind. Ever since we moved here, you've been losing the plot. You changed and I don't know what happened to the wonderful woman that I moved here with, but..." He shook his head and stopped mid-sentence. "You've changed. That's all I'm trying to say."

Losing the plot. Was that it? He really wanted me to believe that?

"It was there," I said. "I could see where the writing had gone through. Where you had written the…"

Dan cut in before I could finish speaking.

"I haven't written anything, Ella. Okay? Let's just get that straight once and for all. I haven't written anything. These notes that keep *appearing*… don't you think it's strange that you always seem to be the one to find them?"

"No, I think that *I* keep finding them because *you* keep leaving them."

Dan moved slowly towards me, as though walking to a wounded animal.

"How many times can I tell you? It's all in your head. You're an intelligent woman, El. You might hide behind your crappy series of nothing jobs, but I know you're smarter than that. You won't settle because you're scared, and I know you're scared now, here with me. I know, Ella, do you not think I know?"

He was sitting on the edge of the bed by that point.

It took everything I had not to lean in towards him and let him hold me. That was all I wanted, to be held. To be understood.

Instead, I snapped back.

"I'm scared of what you're doing to me," I said. Despite how much I wanted him, my mixed-up mess of an insecure psyche was fighting it to the last.

Rather than rise to my bait, Dan reached a hand out.

"It's okay, Ella. Everything is okay. I'm not going to hurt you. I'm never going to hurt you. What reason would I have to do anything to you?"

His warm hand came to rest on the goose-bumped skin of my arm, but instead of feeling reassuring, it threw me further into outrage.

"I'd say there are a few hundred thousand reasons right here."

With those words, he moved away, pushing so hard at my arm that I fell back on the bed, into my pillows. It was hardly domestic violence, but it felt like an attack.

"Man, you can be a bitch, Ella," he said, getting to his feet. "I'm trying so hard here, and I'm putting up with a lot from you. I knew it wasn't going to be an easy ride with you, after all you've been through. I knew when I met you that you were hiding from… from everything. From feelings. From feeling anything. I thought… I thought if I had this reason, this excuse to drive the two of us together here, I thought we could make it work. If we lived together, you'd have to start opening up to me. I always loved you, El. Right from the days of pizza in bed, with nowhere else to go, I knew you were different from anyone I'd ever met before. That's what makes you special. That's what makes you *you*. But since we came here, you've been going out of your mind. Can't you see that?"

I sat, dazed, listening to the words. I had none of my own, none that meant anything.

It had been different with Dan; he was right about that. I was so fixated on the fact that we had been thrown together by the move back to Bittersweet that I'd not even stopped to think about the possibility that he just wanted to be with me. I'd thought that no one had wanted to be with me, though. Why would Dan be any different?

The money, the value of Bittersweet, gave an apparent motive for someone to inveigle their way into my life. So filled with self-doubt, that was all I had seen.

But the notes. The notes.

Even if I didn't have the page with the imprint, I had the note. I turned my gaze from Dan and reached back into the draw, shuffling through the contents.

"What are you doing?"

"The notes. The notes are real," I said.

"Ella, stop," he told me, as I carried on.

My hands scrabbled over the bed, trying to find where I'd left it. I couldn't see it anywhere.

"My phone," I breathed in a triumphant sigh.

"Ella…"

I snapped open the messenger app and showed him.

"Look. I took a photo of it. *Get out.*" I'd half-expected that the message would have been deleted, somehow missing from my phone, but there it was.

"Yes," Dan said, a vein of sadness running through his tone. "I saw it, El. I wasn't even here when that note appeared, was I?"

"Well, you were at work. You left it on the kitchen door for me to find… You…"

He was shaking his head, slowly, as though he were the one in pain.

"Why would you think this of me? Why, Ella? All I've ever done is help you and be good to you. I've tried so hard to be good to you…"

By then he was rising to his feet, backing away from me, in an almost slow-motion reversal of when he had sat down.

"You wanted the house. You never wanted me."

"What are you saying? Ella, have you completely lost your mind?"

Somewhere in that mind, a memory echoed. My dad, standing in this same room, shouting at my mum.

Caitlin, have you completely lost your mind?

Dan's anguished face wasn't that of someone that wanted to cause me harm. Had I been wrong all along?

"The house. It's the house. It's not you, it's the house…"

155

Dan gave one final shake of his head.

"This is too much, Ella. You need help. Tomorrow, I'm taking the day off. I'm going to take you to the doctor and get this sorted out once and for all."

I opened my mouth to speak, and he raised a hand to silence me. A stop sign, clear and unmistakable.

"You need help," he repeated.

And whatever help I needed, I knew he was right.

TWENTY-THREE

When I blamed the house, I knew that there was no logic to those words, but something inside me truly believed that Bittersweet itself had some role in everything that was happening. Not just because I couldn't rationally pinpoint any culprit apart from Dan, but also because the darkness there hadn't begun with him. My childhood, my mother and father, all my life had been tainted by Bittersweet Acres and what had happened there.

I needed help, but I had needed help for a long time.

I needed help when my dad was drip-feeding my mum with ideas that drove her to the edge.

I needed help when she took herself over that edge, because it was a better option for her than trying to carry on living with him.

I needed help afterwards, when Dad and I were alone, and I was the only outlet for his uncontrollable bitterness and malice.

I had always needed help.

Bittersweet Acres was an embodiment of my past and going back, hoping that there was some way that I could re-sculpt that bleak landscape into a fairy tale setting, had been a heinous mistake. There was no happy-ever-after for me there. I couldn't change anything. I could only find more pain and misery.

The house was a black shell, a cold empty corpse. Somehow, it had lured me back. How could I have let that happen? How could I ever have thought that it could ever be wrangled into a happy, positive place? I *was* out of my mind.

And Dan?

Had he really wanted the two of us to be together, or was his motive financial from the outset?

Was he trying to do to me what Dad did to Mum, or was it all in my head after all?

There were so many questions, but only one logical answer: I needed help.

Dan was looking at me, waiting for a response.

You need help, he had said.

I nodded, and as I did so, tears started to flood from my eyes. I let out a howling sob and grabbed hold of Dan.

"I'm so sorry," I said, without really knowing what I was apologising for. "Dan, I don't know what's going on anymore. I don't know what's real or what I'm imagining. I wish I never came back to this hellhole."

"Shh," he said, as he pressed his palms against my back in a tight embrace. "Shh, it's okay, Ella. We're going to make everything okay."

"What's wrong with me?" I choked out the words between heaving sobs. "Why do I ruin everything?"

"It's not your fault," Dan said. "I shouldn't have talked you into this. I didn't realise how hard it would be for you, coming here. I'm sorry, El."

"I'm such a mess." Once I started with the negativity, I couldn't stop. I was spinning out of control, blaming myself for the situation I had so willingly strode into. I knew I was swinging from one extreme to another: everything was Dan, it was all the house, it was me, me, me.

"I do need help," I said, drawing back and looking him in the eyes. My tears blurred his image, and he reached to wipe them with the corner of his sleeve.

"That's okay, El. I'm here for you. We'll get through this. You're going to be okay."

I wanted, so desperately, to believe him, but I couldn't trust him.

I forced my mouth into a tight-lipped smile and withdrew from his hold.

Dan must have sensed the change in energy, because he stood up and stepped away from me, leaving me sitting on the bed.

"Get some rest tonight," he said. "I'll bring you some food…"

I shook my head. I still had that bubbling feeling of nausea; I couldn't have eaten anything.

"… I'll bring you some water then. Make sure you've taken some tablets. You want some now?"

I managed a nod.

"Okay. Then try not to keep going over those thoughts, El."

I knew what he meant, but I didn't know how to do what he was telling me. How could I not think about everything that was happening?

"Okay," I lied.

"I'm going to take the morning off tomorrow and get you down to the doctor, all right?"

"He said…" I was about to tell Dan about how unhelpful Wilson had been when I'd seen him the week before, but that only made me remember how everything had escalated since then. Instead I stopped, and said, "Thank you."

Dan bent to kiss me on top of my head and walked out of the room.

Bittersweet Acres. It's all your fault.

But the house could say nothing. The house could do nothing. And I was alone with my thoughts.

I must have drifted off to sleep, because when I opened my eyes, they focused on something familiar on the bedside table.

Dan had brought my water in Mum's old mug.

For a split second, I felt a rush of anger that he would use that particular cup. I fought against the feeling, making excuses for him. He must have known that it was hers, and perhaps he hoped that would be a comfort to me. If he couldn't make me feel better, maybe he thought she could.

If she had been there, she would have made me feel better.

She always did.

If she had been there, I wouldn't have been going through everything that I was.

I pushed that thought away and took the mug in my hand.

It was almost empty. Even though I didn't remember drinking the water that had been inside it, there were only a couple of mouthfuls left. I drained those dregs and kept hold of the mug, tracing my finger over the letters. MUM.

Her lips had touched the edge of that cup so many times. The same lips that had kissed my forehead when she tucked me into bed at night. All those bedtime stories and the songs she would sing to me. All that love.

After she had gone, I took that mug out of the cupboard time and again. I would hold it in my hands, feeling its fragility, the lightness of it in my grasp. Every time, I would lift it back up, and push it to the back of the cupboard, behind the other cups, where Dad wouldn't pull it out, never use it, never break it. He had tried to remove every trace of her, but he couldn't.

He never broke the mug, but he broke her.

My tears were falling again, and I knew it was no good for me.

I set the mug back onto the bedside table and pulled myself down beneath the cover.

If Mum had got the help that she needed, everything would have different.

I'd come here for her. Perhaps she was telling me that I needed to get help now.

Even before I'd returned to Bittersweet, my life was a mess. I was a mess. If she had drawn me back to give me the kick I needed to finally get help, it had worked. I was ready.

I couldn't change the past. I wasn't going to be able to change Bittersweet, but I could at least try to change myself.

My eyes never left the mug until I faded back into the dark embrace of slumber.

All these things, mugs, lunches, notes, they felt so trivial, but they were everything. It was the little things that mattered. Wasn't that always the way?

TWENTY-FOUR

I woke early in darkness, and immediately knew there was something wrong. Through my sleep-daze, it took me a few moments to come round and get to grips with my surroundings. Everything was out of place.

I was not in my bed; I knew that for sure. The light was different, somehow. There was an icy draft blowing over me from beneath the door. The door was not my bedroom door. I was not in the bedroom.

Little by little, my brain made the connections, trying to make sense of what was happening.

I was not in my bed. I wasn't even in the house at all.

A wave of panic swept over me, and I scrambled to sit up, open my eyes, and take in my surroundings. Where was I and how had I got there? Although it was dark, sharp shards of light pierced the surrounding walls. It was a cell, some kind of cell. Someone had taken me in the night, drugged me and somehow left me alone, trapped.

"Hey!" I yelled. "Hey!"

But even as I was shouting, things became clearer. The walls of the cell came into focus, dark as they were. The wooden slats, the dirt floor upon which I had been sleeping, the rickety door that I had opened so many times before.

I was in the chicken barn.

I didn't know how the hell I had got there, but I was in the chicken barn.

Through my panic, as I pushed my hands into the ground and drew myself to a stooping standing position, I realised something. My head was no longer pounding with the pain that had consumed it for the past few days. Even though I had found myself abandoned in a fog of confusion, there was that one positive to cling onto.

I still felt the undertone of a dull ache, like the afterpain you feel in your leg after an attack of cramp – an echo reminder of the severe agony that was there before. That was nothing, though. That was fine.

I scrabbled to the door and pushed against it with all of my force, expecting it to be barricaded on the other side. If someone had wanted to keep me a prisoner there, surely, they would have secured the exit. I found, as I burst through and landed on the ground, falling awkwardly onto my left arm in a way that sent a lightning bolt of pain through my body, that whoever had put me in the barn wasn't worried about me getting up and leaving.

I didn't know if that was better or worse.

Was someone watching, waiting for me to step outside, ready to pounce?

I still wasn't thinking clearly. This vague idea of a *someone* wasn't fully formed.

The only other person around was Dan.

I let the thought sink in as I pulled myself to my feet.

My thin cotton pyjamas were no protection against the freezing bluster sweeping in from the moors. I wrapped my arms gingerly around myself, rubbing at my aching left limb as I did.

The only other person around was Dan.

I stood, looking down the field towards Bittersweet, not moving despite the biting cold.

I was in the chicken shed. I didn't remember anything. My head was no longer in pain.

He'd drugged me. It was the only answer.

He'd given me a sedative that had knocked me out, and somehow, as a welcome side effect, stopped my head from aching. There were things that could do that, surely? Never having drugged anyone, I didn't know for sure, but my brain was assured by its own speculation.

How could he have? I would have noticed if he'd slipped me something, wouldn't I?

All the headache pills I'd taken over the past few days. He brought me those innocent-looking tablets, the tablets that I thought might make me feel better, but never seemed to work. Had they been painkillers at all? Was I just opening my hand, throwing them into my mouth, and mindlessly going along with his plan?

Everything was starting to make sense, and if what I was thinking was true, I was in serious danger.

I didn't have my phone. I had no idea what time it was, but the field was dark, the sun hadn't yet risen. And I was tired, so tired, but that could have been the knock-on effect of the drug that I had convinced myself I'd been given.

Was Dan in the house, in bed? Could I go back knowing that he was there and suspecting what he had done? If he had done this, I needed to get away and get to the police.

I needed my phone. I needed help.

Barefoot and wearing only one light cotton layer, it wasn't going to happen. My next best option was to creep into the house, get my phone without him seeing me, and make the call instead. The police would come for me, and I would be safe.

My frozen legs had already started to carry me down the slope of the field towards the house. The windows were unlit behind their bars; if he was awake, there was no sign of it.

Why would he do this?

I asked myself the question and answered it almost immediately.

He's trying to tip you over the edge.

The notes, your lunch, hell, maybe even that incessant *pad, pad, pad*. It's all part of one elaborate plan.

But why? Why would he…?

I found an answer before I had even thought of the question that time. I remembered the accusation I'd thrown at him.

Because it was never you that he wanted, it was Bittersweet Acres. He wants you out of there. He wants the house for himself.

No. I thought. *No, no, no.*

But at the same time, it made perfect sense.

Walking down the hill with the freezing wind on my face, my mind felt clearer than it had at any time during the previous two weeks. It was as though Bittersweet had somehow muffled my ability to think, and to see Dan for what he was. Him and the house, co-conspirators, just as Dad and the house had been.

My bare feet stumbled through mud, and the stone-flecked ground pecked at their soles. I could barely see where I was walking in the night's dimness. When I was a kid, the absolute darkness at Bittersweet was one of the things I loved about living there. The night stars seemed so much brighter without the pollution of the city's glow intruding on them. Now, though, I longed for the closeness of other houses, their light, their people.

When I finally made it to the front of Bittersweet, again I expected the door to be locked, just as I had thought the chicken shed would be. I placed my hand onto the cold metal of the handle and gingerly pushed downwards, leaning into it.

It opened.

We had both agreed never to leave the house unlocked, but there it was. My conflicted mind was both angry and pleased. There was no way I could have broken into Bittersweet if it were locked. Dad had made sure that it was impenetrable. Keeping us safe, he said, but keeping us trapped was the truth.

As I pushed the door open, I heard the jingle of metal on metal. There was a bunch of keys hanging from the keyhole on the inside of the house.

There was no way I could be mad at Dan for this; the keys were mine.

TWENTY-FIVE

Of course, the keys meant nothing. Dan could easily have opened the door using mine and left them hanging there. He knew they were always in the same place; it wouldn't be difficult for him to set this up.

I hardly had need for a bunch anyway. The front door key, a spare for a suitcase I only used to move house, a locker key for the office I hadn't been back to in how many days?

Instinctively, as soon as I crept through the door, I turned to lock it behind me. Only as my hand grasped the cold metal did I stop. What if he wanted me to lock myself in here with him? Why would I do that? Wasn't there more danger *inside* this house than out there? I let the keys slip from my fingers, but left the bunch hanging in the lock.

Just in case, I thought.

In case of what, I didn't know.

I stepped as quietly as I could along the hallway. My phone was upstairs by the bed, as far as I knew. I'd like to say that I always plugged it in overnight, but I remembered that earlier in the week I'd somehow forgotten. Half of me hoped that this was one of those times, that I would find it by the sink in the bathroom, or at least somewhere that I wouldn't have to creep past Dan to grab hold of it. The other half of me just wanted the security of knowing that I would be able to find it, and that it would be fully charged.

I needed that phone. I needed help.

Looking up the stairs, I paused to catch my breath and to think about my plan.

Was there another way? Could I walk down to the nearest houses, bang on a door, get help from them instead?

My feet were already bloody, and I was shivering from the struggle through the bitter cold. I was just as likely to collapse on my way. It was too far, and I was too weak. Getting the phone was my only option.

I'd left a trail of blood-flecked dirt across the carpet from the front door. Although I was being as stealthy as I could, I was leaving tracks.

It doesn't matter, I told myself. *Get the phone and get out.*

Get out.

I almost heard the echo of the words on the note that I'd found. It made sense. It all made sense.

I knew the house. I knew its weaknesses. I knew which stairs creaked as someone stood on them, and which I could safely step on as I made my way up. Still, I trod as lightly as I could, both to keep my movements quiet and to reduce the pressure on my aching feet. I couldn't use the banister to support myself; I knew it would creak under my weight. Instead, I pressed my hand against the wall, guiding my way through the dimness. The last thing I wanted was to slip and tumble down.

Halfway up, I mis-stepped, letting my weight fall onto the left side of a stair that I knew I should have avoided. To me, the sound was a deafening creak, and I stumbled slightly, falling forward in my shock. I managed to get my hands in front of me in time to steady myself, but I stopped there, motionless, listening for any sign that my screw up had woken Dan.

All I could hear were my own heavy breaths, and I tried to slow them, to keep them under control. There was no noise from the bedroom, which was reassuring until a thought hit me: what if he wasn't there? Would he really have left me out in the barn and then come back here to the house, my house, and got into bed, my bed?

He hadn't locked me up there; he hadn't locked the door to keep me out of the house. Would he really have made it so easy for me to come back here and find him?

I started to panic.

I hadn't exactly been calm before then, but once I let myself think, my thoughts spiked a burst of adrenaline that instantly heightened my senses and made my heart pound so quickly that I could feel the fluttering jitter throughout my body.

Get the phone and get out. Get the phone and get out.

That was all I had to do.

I took one deep breath, and then another, letting them out as quietly as I could. Focusing my attention forwards, I stood, and started back up the stairs.

Get the phone.
Get out.

When I reached the landing, I saw that the bedroom door was cracked open. Beyond, the room was dark and I couldn't tell whether or not Dan was in the bed. I was relieved, though, that I wouldn't have to go through the effort of trying to open that door without making a sound. Even if he were there, perhaps I could sneak inside and grab my phone without alerting him to my presence.

If he caught me, what would he do? What lengths was he prepared to go to?

I didn't want to think about it. I couldn't. He had made himself out to be so caring. He wanted to be there for me, to help me. That's what he had said, but then, this. I couldn't trust him. At that point, I couldn't even trust myself.

I didn't know what was happening to me.

I just knew that I needed to get out of there.

TWENTY-SIX

I stepped inside the bedroom and had to hold back a relieved yelp as I saw my phone. It was there, plugged into the charger, on the bedside table. If Dan had thought ahead, surely he would have moved it, unplugged it at the very least, but he'd been careless. The phone was right there, within reach.

Dan was asleep, in his usual position, facing towards the window, away from me. Could it be so easy?

I padded tip-toe across to the table and plucked my phone from the cable. My hands were sticky against its case, and it almost slipped to the floor.

Careful, I told myself. *Careful now*.

I could creep my way back downstairs, get out of earshot, or make the call right there.

Dan was going to get what was coming to him, and I was going to be safe.

I watched the rise and fall of his body as he snored lightly, and then turned my attention back to the phone.

Let him hear. Let him know what was coming.

I pressed the button three times in succession.

999

Without pausing, I clicked the phone icon to make the call.

Dan shuffled, almost imperceptibly, at the sound.

I held the phone to my ear, watching him. A warm flood raced through my veins, like a shot of vodka making its way around my system.

The call connected.

"999 emergency. Which service do you require?"

"Hello," I said. "Police."

Then I heard his voice.

"El. What are you doing?"

Dan had rolled over and was looking straight at me.

I scrambled to my feet and ran for the landing.

"Ella. Stop."

He was up and behind me, too fast, too strong.

"Ma'am are you all right? I'm connecting your call now."

"Yes," I panted. "Thanks."

Before I could reach the top of the stairs, his arms were around me, and he grabbed my phone, ending the call.

"They'll phone back," I yelped. "That's what they do. If I don't talk to them, they'll come here, anyway. They'll come, Dan."

I kicked out at him, and he kept me tightly in his grasp.

"You need to stop. Right now. Stop."

"Let go of me." My legs were swinging off the ground; Dan was carrying me back to the bedroom.

"Listen, just chill, okay? Talk to me. You don't need to phone the police. We can work this out, El."

My feet were aching, my body was exhausted and my heart was breaking.

"I told you. Tomorrow I'm taking you to get help."

"I need help now. I need someone to help me get away from you."

As he set my feet on the ground, my phone started to ring.

He looked me up and down, his eyes falling on my feet.

"Where have you been? What have you done? What's going on, Ella?"

"You know," I sobbed. "You shut me in the shed. You…"

He shook his head.

"No, no, no."

The phone was still ringing. I had to answer.

Dan released his grip on me just enough to wrestle the phone into his hand and click the accept call button and pass the handset to me. The hesitance in his action was obvious.

"Don't," he mouthed. "Please."

"Hello? Police," said the voice at the other end of the phone.

I looked into Dan's eyes.

"Ma'am. Your call was disconnected. Do you need assistance?"

Dan shook his head again.

"Yes," I said, and I saw Dan's shoulders sink.

He took a step away and fell back onto the bed.

I inhaled sharply and spoke again. "But I don't need the police. I'm so sorry to waste your time."

I heard Dan groan slightly.

"Are you sure, Ma'am?" the voice said.

I wasn't sure. I wasn't sure about anything. I had no idea what was happening.

Don't blame him.

Get out.

I shook my head, trying to focus.

"Yes," I said, trying to mask my uncertainty.

"If you change you mind, call back anytime, Ma'am."

"Thanks," I said. "And I'm sorry."

I clicked to end the call, and stood, motionless.

"Why didn't you get them to come out here?" Dan said calmly, still lying on the bed.

"Because I…" What? I wasn't even sure.

"You know it wasn't me, don't you? I didn't take you out there. I didn't even know that you'd got up until I heard you making that phone call, Ella."

I stared at him in disbelief.

"You get up every night, El. You wander around the house. You've obviously been leaving those notes for yourself, raiding the fridge, doing who knows what else."

"W-what?" I stuttered.

"I guess this time you wandered out of the house. You're not safe, Ella. You're not safe anymore."

I didn't feel safe. I knew I wasn't safe.

"I haven't… I didn't…"

Dan pulled himself back up to a sitting position and patted the bed next to him.

"Come here," he said.

I paused, weighing up the consequences of my next decision.

"Come on," he repeated.

My torn feet begged me to accept, and I flopped beside him.

"Dan, what's happening to me?"

"You're not safe." He gently turned me to look at him. "I think you're having a breakdown."

A terrifying sound came from the core of my body, out through my mouth as a long wail.

I couldn't control it. The anguish tore through me.

Since I moved back to Bittersweet, everything had gone downhill. My world was crumbling around me. I felt helpless and lost, and I didn't know what to do. I was stuck in a never-ending cycle of despair and I couldn't find a way out.

Was I having a breakdown? Was that what it was?

Or was Dan playing his game perfectly?

TWENTY-SEVEN

Against my better judgement, I let the pain in my body dictate my next move. I lay in the bed, shrugging off Dan's arms as he tried to spoon me, and tried to sleep.

I'd had my chance to escape, to get out of there, and I let it slip through my fingers. I chose to believe in the possibility that it was I who was at fault, not Dan. I'd been the common denominator in everything that had ever gone wrong in my life. There was every chance that Dan was right.

I swung from the absolute belief that he was manipulating me and using me to the terrible and tragic hope that there was something wrong with me.

Despite saying that he was taking the day off to get me to the doctor, when I woke, I was alone. The space in the bed beside me was empty and cold. Dan had been gone for some time.

I reached over to that bedside time to grab my phone and check the time, but my hand came back empty. The surface was clear; no phone.

At once, everything came flooding back to me. The sleepless night, waking up in the dirt of the chicken barn, almost getting the police up there. The memories swam, dreamlike, as though they didn't belong to me.

My phone. Where had I left it?

I'd told the call operator that I didn't want the police, and that I was okay, and then? Then I'd let myself fall onto the bed.

I patted around on the duvet, and shook it, hoping to dislodge my phone, but again, my search came up with nothing. It had definitely been there, so where was it now?

Dan was gone. My phone was gone.

The truth hit me like a slap in the face: I had made a terrible mistake.

"Dan?" I called out his name, but I knew already there would be no reply. He'd never meant to help me. All he wanted was to stop me from calling the police. He would have said anything. He hardly had to say a word. I'd given in without a fight, just like I always had. Just like Mum before me always had. I'd turned out to be the same weak woman that she was.

I'm sorry, I mumbled.

I was sorry for having those thoughts about Mum when I loved her so much, missed her so much, and wished more than anything that she had been stronger. But I did have those thoughts, because they were true. She was weak. I was weak. And look where it had got me: in exactly the same situation she had been in.

That jittering feeling of panic trembled through my body again, and I leapt from the bed.

I pushed against the door and felt the jolting resistance as it refused to budge. It was locked.

It was locked.

Dan had locked me in the bedroom.

I howled a long no, a scream of disbelief, but hadn't it always been inevitable that this would happen?

Bittersweet was forcing me to relive the same screwed up series of events that Mum had gone through with Dad. The doors had locks, and the windows had bars for a reason: he had used them. We were his prisoners then, and now I'd found myself in that same situation again.

At first, Dad had banished Mum to the bedroom. He would send her upstairs like a naughty child for hours at a time to sit and think about the things she had said or done to offend him.

His tea was too milky: an hour in the bedroom.

His shirt had a crease after she was meant to have ironed it: two hours to reflect on that.

She'd spoken when he was trying to listen to the news: take the rest of the night alone upstairs.

Then the same punishments were extended to me.

Mum would be cloistered in my parents' room, and I in mine, separated by the landing, and the two doors that kept us apart, isolated.

I sat out my sentences at first, but as I grew older, the penalties became harsher. I wasn't just sent to my room; I had to sit on my bed, without moving, for hours on end. I knew he could come and check on me at any time, that if I was on the floor, on my chair, at my desk, the punishment would go beyond the imprisonment. He was a man of mental, rather than physical cruelty, my father, but that didn't mean that he couldn't cross the line.

Two weeks after my sixteenth birthday, I had my first date with a boy. Not that I'd never been interested in anyone before, but no one had been interested in me. It was a lad from school, someone I'd got talking to after class. Nothing memorable, no big story behind it. We were just two kids hanging out; neither of us experienced enough or stupid enough to do anything more than talk, laugh and peck each other on the lips at the end of it all. But I hadn't told Dad where I was, of course, or who I was with.

That wasn't the problem, though. I'd hidden my whereabouts, covered up my companion. I thought everything was fine. Until I got home five minutes after curfew.

Those five minutes were the difference between my ability to have happy memories of my first date and what actually happened instead. I don't even know how I let it happen, but I walked through the front door at five past seven to find Dad standing in the hallway, staring straight at me. He must have been waiting there for me to arrive back, dead still, watching, patiently watching.

I heard Mum yelp from the living room through the closed door.

"Leave her alone," she shouted. "You leave her alone."

Dad didn't break eye contact. He stood silently as I closed the door behind me.

"I'm sorry…" I began, but he cut me off with a swift slap across my face.

"No!" My mum must have heard the impact of skin on skin. She yelled from the living room, but she didn't run out to help me. Even in the shock of him striking me, I wondered why she'd kept her distance.

"After everything I've done for you. Everything I've given you. Everything I've given up."

I didn't know what he was talking about. It was Mum that made the sacrifices. I couldn't think of a single thing that Dad had done for me. Not one.

"Please, don't," I heard Mum calling from the living room. She started to bang on the door, and it was then that I knew. He'd locked her in there.

"Dad…?" I asked so many questions with that one word.

"I have spent my life in this house, in this ridiculous, pathetic life for you." He spat the last word, the flecks of his spittle landing on my face.

I didn't flinch. It would only have angered him.

"I never wanted this. I never wanted you. Everything I've ever done has been for her…" He pointed towards the locked door. "…and for you."

The evening had turned from one of the happiest to incontestably the worst for the sake of five minutes.

I stood my ground and listened as the words slammed into me. His resentment stung harder than the slap had.

He didn't touch me again, after that night, but there were many more locked doors: me in one room, Mum in another. Each time we were left for longer. The misery of each of us knowing what the other was going through was worse than any physical trauma.

Getting to the bedroom door and finding that Dan had locked it was the deepest betrayal, and a horrific echo of my miserable past.

"No!" I screamed again, "No!"

TWENTY-EIGHT

When Dad had locked us in our rooms, he had always been downstairs. He never left the house when we were imprisoned. The thought of him below, going about his usual routines – television and snacks, vodka and the newspaper – while we were locked away somehow made the punishment worse. My feelings were meaningless. I was worthless to him.

He had never wanted me.

I didn't know for sure, but I couldn't hear any sound from the ground floor. It seemed that Dan had left the house.

I would never have dared try to escape Dad's punishments, but this was different. I wasn't being punished; I had done nothing wrong. Dan had locked me up because he was a sick, twisted man. He had conned me, talked me around time and time again, and he had left me there, locked in that room.

I wasn't going to be there when he returned. I was getting out, and then I was doing what I should have done the night before: I was going to call the police.

I was in danger; I knew that much. How far was Dan prepared to go?

One thing was certain: I didn't want to wait to find out.

I didn't have a key to the bedroom door, of course. I'd never had a key. Where Dan had found it, I didn't know. Perhaps he had always had it, ever since we moved in, waiting for his chance to trap me. Perhaps everything had been building to this.

There had to be a way out. If he wasn't waiting down there for me, I had a chance.

What to do though? I'd never broken free before, but only because I knew it would only lead to harsher punishment.

I had to pick the lock. That was the only way.

I needed something to help me. I looked around, but nothing stood out.

Without thinking, I stuck my hands into my pyjama pockets, feeling about for anything I could use.

My fingers came into contact with the edge of a scrap of paper. Had I left one of those stupid notes in there? I pulled it out and sucked in a sharp breath as I read what was written on it.

This wasn't one of the notes I'd previously read; this was a fresh piece of hell.

Two words, that was all.

Two words.

Dead soon.

I dropped it on the floor as though it had burned my fingers.

What the…?

I stood above the note, looking down at the by now familiar looping letters.

Dead soon.

My head was already bursting with the flashing firework show behind my eyes. Bending to read those letters didn't help at all.

It was a threat, of course. How Dan had planted it there without waking me up was a mystery.

Drugs, I thought again. *He's obviously drugging me.*

I'd tried to avoid the truth before, but then, it seemed inescapable.

The headaches. The drugs. The mental manipulation. Dan had started his regime of torment as soon as we had moved to Bittersweet. I'd been too stupid to realise.

And when I had let myself consider it, every time I had fallen foul of his lame excuses and false promises. I hated how gullible and ridiculously foolish I had been.

When I thought it through, when I really thought about it, there were only two explanations for what had been happening. Either he was trying to make me think I was crazy or he was trying to kill me.

The one thing I know for sure is that I need to get out of this house.

After everything that happened there, I should never have gone back. I let him talk me into it. I gave up so easily, and for what?

I got myself into this and now, I either get myself out of it or I find out which of the explanations is correct.

Dead soon.

Not if I could help it.

I had been foolish. Time and time again, I had been fooled.

My life was on the line, and I had to get out.

Get out had turned out to be a prescient warning. If *dead soon* was equally accurate, I had to take heed.

Get out.

Get out.
Get out.

Whenever I had been locked in my room before, I knew Mum was there, along the landing, locked in too. Neither one of us was punished without the other receiving the same sentence. Now, though, Mum was long gone, and there was only me, alone in my prison.

We had never escaped from those rooms before because we had never dared to. Dad was always waiting, even if we had managed somehow.

Now I was almost sure that I was in the house alone. If I could make it out of the bedroom, there was every chance I could be free.

What chance *did* I have, though? Dad had barred the windows when Mum had risked her life to try to climb out on one of the early occasions we had been incarcerated. We were lucky then that he hadn't left us there in the house, because I was sure that she would have gone through with the jump if he hadn't run in to stop her.

She was desperate, not suicidal. Six hours in that room, no food, no water, no idea when he was going to let her out again; she wanted out. I'd been asleep. That was my way of coping when he shut us away. There was nothing else to do, so while Mum paced and stressed about the two of us being on lockdown, I slept it out.

Hearing Dad crash through the bedroom door, yelling at Mum to *stop, stop, stop* was what woke me.

I didn't know at the time, of course, what was happening, but when the bars went up two days later, I figured it out.

It's for your safety, was what he told me, but I knew that wasn't true.

I wished I'd made Dan rip those bars down before I even stepped back into Bittersweet Acres.

I wished I'd never stepped back into Bittersweet Acres at all.

If Mum had been with me, we would have found a way. Regardless of the bars, the locks, the space between us, I was sure we could have worked out how to get out of there.

But Mum wasn't with me. She was long gone, and now Bittersweet had me, only me, alone, and trapped.

TWENTY-NINE

Not for the first time, I was wrong.

Mum was always with me.

The thought stopped me in my tracks. Mum.

Slowly, I reached my hand up to the side of my head.

My hair clip – Mum's hair clip – wasn't there.

When was the last time I had worn it? I'd been so distracted, so far from my usual self for the past few days, I couldn't remember when I'd seen it.

Spinning, I raced to the bedside table. I tore through the drawers, tossing out everything that came into my hands. Painkillers, pens, scraps of paper, tissues. I threw them all to the floor. It had to be in there somewhere.

I emptied the drawer down to the wooden base and let out a howl of frustration when I reached the bottom. It wasn't there.

In Dan's drawer? I couldn't see why it would be, but I was ruling nothing out. I scurried to his side of the bed and pulled back the handle. His drawer was empty.

Completely empty. There were a few of his things scattered on top – his phone charger, a coaster, a receipt from the supermarket – but no sign of my hair clip.

Turning, I scanned the room.

Please let it be here.

I dug into the washing basket, fishing for anything I might have worn in the past few days, pockets that could be concealing what I was searching for. I'd mostly stayed in my pyjamas; I wasn't holding out much hope. There were T-shirts, shirts, underwear. At the bottom, I found my hoodie. I'd been wearing it only a couple of days ago. Optimism bloomed in my mind, but as I stuck my hands into the pockets, disappointment took over. Empty.

Please, please, please.

Falling to my hands and knees, I peered under the wardrobe. It was dusty; the cleaners I had hired clearly hadn't done as thorough of a job as they had charged me for. I sneezed, an impulse as much as an effect of the dirt, and pulled back. There was nothing there.

Finally, I crawled, almost out of options, almost out of hope, to the bed.

Taking a deep breath, I bent to look beneath it.

There, right under its centre, I could see a small object. It had to be my clip. It had to be. I was at the foot of the bed, and as I reached my hand into the dark space, I realised it was too far from me. I shuffled around to the side and tried again. Still, it was out of reach. I stretched until my fingertips were less than an inch from my target, but that was not enough.

Shit.

I thought for a split second and withdrew my arm, spinning round so that my legs were facing the bed.

This has got to work.

I was saying the words out loud, letting my thoughts into the room, focussed on the task at hand.

Sliding forward, I slipped my legs beneath the bed.

I may be short, but my legs were long enough to reach. I felt the metal against my left sole and kicked hard, sending it flying across the floor, skidding to the other side of the room.

Yes!

I yelped the triumphant word and yanked myself backwards. My pyjamas were grey-fluffed with the under-bed dust, but I couldn't have cared less.

I raced around the bed and picked up my prize.

The hair grip. My mum's hair grip. My hair grip.

I had it. And I was sure that this was going to be the solution.

It wasn't going to be as easy as that.

Hair grip in hand, I dashed to the door.

Please work, please work.

I repeated the words as I unclipped the fastener and slipped the end into the lock. I didn't know what I was doing. All I could do was hope that the mechanism was so primitive that I'd be able to jimmy it somehow and release the catch.

I wiggled the metal prong. Never had I wanted a YouTube video more than that moment. I was sure that if I could look up how to pick a lock, I would have been out of there in no time. I should have brushed up on all those life skills when I had the chance. Sure, I could unblock a drain, but what about really useful things like being able to escape when someone locks you in your bedroom?

All I had for reference were memories of movies. The terrified heroine, trapped against her will, with only minutes left to escape.

I had to get out of there before Dan came back. I couldn't bear to imagine what wicked plans he was brewing. Locking me up was bad, but there could be worse to come. I had to open that door.

I could feel the end of the clip catching against something, but there was no sign of the release that I was hoping for. I pulled back and looked at the grip. Those beautiful enamel flowers. My mind flashed back to seeing it pinned in Mum's long strawberry blonde hair. I wished I had grown up to be even half as beautiful as she was. All I could hope now was that I was stronger. I wasn't giving up.

Levering the clip up and down, I let myself mumble a semi-prayer.

Please, if you let me get out of this, I'll...

But I didn't have to complete my bargain plea. I jerked backwards as I felt something move inside the lock mechanism.

Let that be it, let that be it.

I repeated the words as though chanting a spell, and turned the door handle. As I pulled, the door opened.

A surge of elation flooded my body. I'd swung from abject hopelessness to the sweet release of freedom, and I felt the rush run through me. My head was drunk-dazed, almost not quite wanting to believe that I had escaped.

I sprinted along the landing and turned the corner at the top of the stairs. I wasn't thinking clearly; my body was driven by my instinct to get out of there. *Get out, get out, get out.*

As I put my foot down onto the top stair, I felt the world give way beneath me. Instead of landing on the wooden step, it slid, launching me forwards in an unplanned somersault. I reached out with my arms, trying to cushion my fall, flapping for something to hold on to, to steady myself.

Those moments stretched like minutes, thoughts racing through my muddled mind. The last thing I remember is the thucking sound of my head colliding with something

that was hard enough to send me spinning
into deep darkness.

THIRTY

I woke in a brightly lit room and had to squint my eyes against the glare. As I started to focus, I could make out a window that I didn't recognise. Waist-height to ceiling; it reminded me of a schoolroom.

But I was lying down. Looking up, looking across, looking around. My surroundings began to become clear. The walls were magnolia, the sheets cheap, thin cotton. I was in a hospital bed. A side room, not one of those curtained corridors.

My head was throbbing, but not with the same ache that I'd been feeling for the past few days. This was a new pain, at the back of my head. I reached up and felt a soft patch, tender to my touch.

I'd fallen. The memories rushed back as I jerked my fingers away from the swollen lump. Had I knocked myself out? How had I got to the hospital?

None of that seemed to matter. I would be safe there. I'd made it away from Bittersweet, away from Dan, and I was never going back.

"She's waking up!"

A man's voice, from the doorway.

I twisted my head, and the thudding pain intensified.

I knew before I saw him whose voice it was.

I hadn't escaped from Dan at all. He was there, in the hospital with me. Still watching, still a threat.

"No!" My throat was dry and word came out as a rasping scrape.

"Ella, it's me," Dan said, sprinting to my bedside.

I tried to sit up, to move away from him, but I was connected to a monitor on one side and a drip on the other. A tube was pronged into my nostrils, restraining me further. I tugged at those tethers as I jerked forwards.

"Help!" My voice was too quiet; shouting was as useless as everything else I'd tried to do to get away.

"What do you need?" Dan spoke as though nothing had happened, like he had never drugged me and locked me in a bedroom.

Wide-eyed with fear, I reached around, trying to find the nurse call button.

"Get away," I hissed, kicking a leg out at Dan.

My hand made contact with the buzzer and I hammered my finger on it.

"Come on, come on, come on."

"Ella? What's the matter? Are you in pain? Your head?"

Dan hadn't taken the hint, as he sat on the edge of the bed, well within range of my kicking leg, and rested his hand on my arm.

"Should I go and get someone for you? Those buzzers are useless."

"What? Uh, yes. Get someone." If he was going to play dumb, I could too. I didn't have a clue what was happening, but I remembered enough to know that it was his fault I was in that bed, and that I needed to get away from him.

Dan got back up on his feet almost as quickly as he'd sat down with me. He looked like a man who didn't know what to do. My mind raced, trying to think two steps ahead of him. To be acting like that, he must have a plan.

He stood in the doorway, looking out into the corridor beyond. Was he going to intercept the nurse? Get his words in before I could tell her what he had done?

I didn't have to wait long to find out.

From my tethered position on the bed, a nurse came into view and stood next to Dan.

"She's awake," he said. "I think she's in pain."

The nurse nodded without speaking to Dan and edged her way past into the room. In a moment of triumph, I realised that whatever Dan's plan was, it hadn't worked.

She leaned over and cancelled the call buzzer.

"Alright, love. Doctor has been waiting for you to wake up. I'll pop along and fetch him."

I thought quickly and muttered words I knew she wouldn't be able to hear.

The nurse bent towards my lips.

"What's that, love?"

Any other day, I would have made a fuss about being called 'love' it was one of those unnecessary terms of endearment strangers used that made me feel unreasonably uncomfortable.

"I need to get out of here," I whispered into her ear.

"Of course," the nurse said, placatingly. "Let's get the doctor in here to see you, all right?"

Before I could protest further, the nurse had picked up the folder from the end of my bed and fluttered back out of the room.

"No!" I called after her, but it was futile.

"Useless," Dan said, watching her walk down the corridor. "The doctor will sort you some pain relief out when he gets here. Missy there is probably late for her tea break or something."

I clenched my teeth and faked a smile. For now, it seemed safer to go along with Dan's deception. Alone in a closed room together, I didn't want to risk angering him. I still didn't know how far he was willing to go to hurt me.

"You gave me quite a scare, El. We're here now, though. Everything is going to be alright."

I wanted to be on my feet and out of the room, but my best hope was to wait out the doctor. The pain from the bump on my head was competing with the throb of my temples. If I had to wait there, I needed to lie back down.

Play along, I told myself. *Be cool and play along.*

I rested my eyes, keeping them open just enough to be able to see through the crack. I hoped I could convince him that I wasn't watching him.

Dan sat back down on the side of my bed, looking down at me, and then turning his gaze over to the door.

We were both playing the waiting game, and this was one game he wasn't going to win.

THIRTY-ONE

Dan had his back to me, but I carried on with the pretence that my eyes were closed, just in case he turned around. Both of us watched the door until it opened again, and a short man in a dark sweater and trousers entered the room.

If it wasn't for his identity badge, I wouldn't have known he was the doctor that we were waiting for. Doctor Cross, I read, before he introduced himself.

"Ella, how lovely to see you awake," he said, before Dan had a chance to speak.

I wasn't wasting any time. I yelled straight away.

"It was him. Get him away from me. It was Dan. It was Dan. It was Dan."

I tried to sit again, stretching towards the doctor, leaning around Dan.

"Help me!"

Doctor Cross gestured for Dan to get up and step aside. He took Dan's place on the bed beside me and calmly rested his hand on my arm.

"It's okay, Ella. You're safe here."

"I'm not safe from him. He was trying to…"

Despite my accusations, Dan stood beside the bed, looking at me.

I thought he would at least say something in his own defence, but he was resolutely silent. Did he think the doctor wouldn't believe me?

"He locked me up. He drugged me. It's all his fault."

The doctor looked at Dan, but only briefly, and then looked back at me.

"Locking you up wasn't, er, ideal. I know that must have been very confusing for you…"

"Confusing?" I burst in. This wasn't the response I'd expected. "Did you hear what I said? He locked me in the bedroom! He was trying to kill me. I know he was. The note…"

I reached down for my pyjama pocket and realised immediately that I was no longer wearing my own clothes. I was in a hospital nightie. No pockets. No note.

Still, false imprisonment was a crime, wasn't it? Why wasn't the doctor *doing* anything?

"It must all be very confusing for you," Cross continued, as if I hadn't spoken. He raised his hand when I opened my mouth to speak again. "Dan has told us about what's been happening. You're lucky that he found you when he did."

"Lucky?" I was incredulous. Whatever he'd told them, it was obviously not the truth. "He was trying to kill me. Can you hear what I'm telling you?"

A terrible thought struck me, and I gulped in a breath.

"Is this… am I in a mental ward? Is this a psychiatric unit? Do you think I'm…" I didn't want to say the word, but I forced it out. "Insane?"

"What?" The doctor actually laughed. "No. Of course not. This is a regular, straight-up medical ward. You've not been here long. We transferred you up from accident and emergency after they were finished with you there."

I wasn't sure I wanted the details, but I was relieved to hear that my mental health wasn't being questioned. If they didn't think I was nuts, they had to believe me. I'd assumed that as soon as I told someone what

Dan had done, it would be game over for him. It wasn't working out that way.

"Look," I said again. "I'm telling you that this man locked me up and…"

"Ella, we know. We know exactly what happened. This man saved your life."

"No," I yelled, even though he was less than two feet away from me. "You're not listening. He was trying to kill me."

"Ella, please." Dan finally spoke. He turned to the doctor. "Can you just explain to her what's happened, so that she stops blaming me?"

Don't blame him.

The words from that note echoed in my aching head. I raised my hand up and touched my temple.

"Is your head still hurting? The headache? Or the, er, injury?"

"Both," I said, more quietly. My words were falling on deaf ears and I was tired, so tired. If Doctor Cross had an explanation, I wanted him to get on with telling me what it was.

"I'll arrange for some more analgesia for you. That should start to get better soon, though. Once your system is clear and…"

So Dan had drugged me? Why was everyone acting so calmly then? Why was he still there?

"Tell me," I said. "What's going on?"

"You've been poisoned," the doctor said, flat and with no emotion. "You're lucky to be alive."

I lashed out towards Dan, tugging so hard that the monitor attached to my finger pinged off and flew back across the room like a bungee.

The doctor jumped to his feet and grabbed my arms, holding me down.

"Ella," he pleaded. "Don't blame him. It wasn't Dan. It wasn't him."

THIRTY-TWO

The look of shock on my face must have been obvious. The doctor released his grip, slightly, as if testing my response. I stayed put.

"If," I stuttered, "If it wasn't Dan…"

It didn't add up.

"It was the house," the doctor said.

If he wasn't a medical professional, looking at me straight-faced as he spoke the words, I would have thought it was a joke.

"The *house*?" The idea had gone through my mind so many times over the previous days, but it had never made enough sense to be a plausible explanation. Dan was trying to make me think I was crazy, or he was trying to kill me. It couldn't possibly have been the house, no matter what this obviously deluded doctor was saying.

He nodded, though.

I looked up at Dan. The look of concerned anxiety on his face was unmistakable. Was he concerned about me, or about the truth that was about to come out?

The doctor spoke again.

"When you were admitted, we treated you for the head wound first. That was the obvious injury. However, it soon became clear that there was something else. The nurse did the routine observations, fastened you up to the monitors, and well, she found something that she wasn't expecting."

I wished that he'd get on with it, and make his point.

"You said I was poisoned."

"And you were. The house was poisoning you. Every day you spent there, the more danger you were in. Dan told us you were hearing noises."

I nodded.

"Then getting headaches?"

"I thought I had the flu. They were unbearable. I couldn't do anything," I said, finally glad I could agree with what was being said. "What about the notes?" I asked.

Dan and the doctor shared an exchange of looks.

"Your boyfriend here told us about how you had started to get up in the middle of the night. He didn't realise that you were sleepwalking at first."

"It all added up, though. Over the past week. You were snacking and forgetting about it. Then you left those notes and couldn't remember doing it."

"I wrote the notes?" I couldn't believe what I was hearing. "No," I said. "I didn't… I…" But was I sure of that? Was I sure of anything?

"When you started to leave the house in the night, Dan here realised that you needed help."

"And I locked the bedroom door to keep you safe while I went to fetch the doctor."

"Couldn't you have phoned him? Did you have to leave me there? What did you think I would do…?"

"I had no idea what you might do, El. I was terrified that you were going to hurt yourself. You were wandering barefoot in the field in the middle of the night, babe. What was I supposed to do?"

"But you could have phoned still?"

"I tried. As soon as the surgery opened I phoned, and that stick up the butt receptionist told me she could fit you in next week. It wasn't soon enough, so I went down there to sort it out. I couldn't risk what you might do on your own, though. I thought you'd be safe in that room. I never meant…"

His expression was filled with genuine remorse, but believing him was a hard stretch.

"And it's a good job he did," the doctor said. "Bumping your head was unfortunate, of course, but Dan has saved your life. If you had stayed in that house, you could have soon been dead."

Dead soon.

If I had been writing the notes for myself, which I still didn't believe, perhaps my subconscious was trying to tell me something.

"That house is a death trap," the doctor said. "No one should have been living there. Dan would have succumbed too, in time. You're much smaller, and apparently less healthy than he is, so…" He shrugged as though the conclusion was obvious. "It acted more quickly on your body."

"What?" I asked, no longer able to maintain my patient front. "What happened to me?"

"Your heating system. Your boiler. It was malfunctioning, probably had been for some time."

"Yes, but what's that got to do with anything?"

"It was leaking carbon monoxide into the house. Usually, if you were in a new build or renting somewhere that had to meet regulations, there would have been a monitor with an alarm to let you know about that kind of thing. But, move into an old farmhouse on a remote hill that's been in your family for decades? No such luck. The system was faulty, and it was slowly killing you."

"The headaches. That makes sense, but… all the things that were happening though? What about the notes, the noises?"

"All symptoms of CO poisoning," the doctor said, shaking his head. "Hallucinations, sleepwalking, memory loss. I dare say your body was trying to get you out of that house when you went wandering."

Get out.

My body, my brain, they were both trying their best to save me. I just hadn't realised it.

"The notes? I wrote them to myself?"

"I believe Dan when he says he didn't write them. He told us about them, you know. He told us everything. He didn't know what was happening to you, and he was scared, Ella."

"Oh, I'm so sorry, Dan. I'm so sorry."

Dan shook his head and gave me the slightest smile.

Bittersweet Acres. It *had* all been the house, after all. The idea had never been as crazy as I thought it was.

From the moment I went back there, it had been killing me.

THIRTY-THREE

Dan visited me each day while I was in hospital. He was staying on a friend's sofa while the heating was fixed back at Bittersweet, but was in no hurry to move back there without me.

I was in no hurry to move back there at all.

I had no idea what was going to happen when I was discharged. For all I knew, I had no home, no job, and perhaps I no longer had Dan either.

I couldn't believe he would stick around after everything I had said.

By the third day, my headache had long since cleared, and the lump I'd gained falling on the stairs was subsiding.

Dan turned up for the allotted visiting period bang on time, and kissed me as soon as he came into my room.

"How are you feeling today?" he asked.

"Better now you're here," I said. "I would say that I'm ready to go home now, but I'm not even sure where home is."

"A couple more days, the nurses say. Be patient, El."

I nodded and pulled him in for a hug. I was free of the constant monitoring by then, and the nurses had disconnected my drip. I didn't know why they were still keeping me there, but I didn't know where else I would go.

"So what happens now?" I asked him.

"We start again," Dan said, as though the answer was obvious.

To me, though, it wasn't. I was assuming nothing.

"Are you sure you still want to be with me? After the way I accused you of…" I couldn't bring myself to say the words. "I've been impossible."

Dan smiled.

"I told you, El. I'm here for you. I want to look after you."

"Well, I don't know about that," I protested. "I'm a strong, independent woman, you know. I don't really need to be looked after. Before I met you I…"

"You had YouTube and Google searches, I know. That's not what I meant. I don't want to look after you in a patronising, coddling kind of way. I just want to be there for you. I want us to be there for each other."

I nodded, understanding the difference.

We did have a future. I didn't know what it was or where we were going to be, but I still had him. Despite everything, I still had him.

After five days on the ward, I could tell the nurses were keen to get rid of me. My headaches had cleared up. There was no more sleepwalking. There were no more notes.

I still had questions, though.

When Doctor Cross came to discharge me, I had to ask the obvious.

"Did Dad… I mean, was Dad poisoned too? What happened to me… did it happen to him?"

Cross shook his head.

"We don't think so. It's hard to tell, though. Looking at the report. Your father, well, his body was not in a good condition when it was discovered. We can only assume that he wasn't a very social man. I won't go into too much detail, but some of the signs that we might have picked up on, well, they were impossible to see. What was clear, though, was that your father was a chronic abuser of alcohol."

"So you just hung it on that, didn't think to look further? Blamed it on the drink? I suppose you think he deserved to die like that."

"We dropped the ball. The decomposition, the... well, you don't need to hear this. I'm sorry that mistakes were made, mistakes that caused you to suffer too. If we could have spotted carbon monoxide poisoning, no one would have been able to move into that house. Not before the dangers had been eliminated."

I couldn't stop shaking my head. It was wrong beyond belief.

It was the first time I had ever jumped to Dad's defence. He *was* an alcoholic, he always had been, but that wasn't all he was. He was my dad, too. No matter what he had done, he was my dad, too. Hadn't I almost followed in those footsteps? I was strong enough to fight my addiction and find my way onto a better path. Not a particularly fulfilling or rewarding path, but at least I had swerved the downward spiral that had done for Dad.

For the first time, I had seen Dad as a person, a regular human being, and not just our tormentor. There were no excuses for how he had treated us, but perhaps in his own twisted way, he *was* trying to keep us safe.

Still, he had driven Mum to her death and had driven me away. I had no love for him, but somehow, I could no longer hate him either.

I had other questions, and I asked them.

"Are there likely to be any long-term effects from my exposure to the carbon monoxide leak?"

I feared ongoing headaches, spacing out, memory loss. I didn't want to wake up in the chicken barn, or worse still on the moors, alone, cold, and lost.

Cross shook his head.

"You appear to have made a full recovery. Neurological tests haven't shown any sign that you're likely to have any ongoing health issues as a result of the exposure."

I let out a long sigh, relieved to hear the good news. I needed some, amidst everything that had happened to me over the past couple of weeks.

"We'll send a note to your GP so he can do a follow up, but that's all you should need. Obviously, if you have any problems at all…" He handed me a sheet of paper and tapped the phone number at the top. "Give us a call."

I doubted he was part of the *us* that would answer if I called, but I gratefully took it, anyway.

"You're sure she's going to be all right?" Dan chipped in.

Cross nodded. "As sure as we can be."

Dan cleared his throat and spoke again. "And me? I'm not going to have any, er, effects either? I was in that house, too."

"You were checked over?" Cross asked, as though he couldn't remember doing it.

"Yes," Dan agreed. "But…" He let his thoughts trail off.

"Bound to be a worry when something like this happens," Cross said, with a cheerful tone. Then he rose to his feet and extended a hand towards Dan. "Best wishes then, and with all good intent, I hope not to see you again."

Dan smiled at the attempted humour and shook his hand; I followed suit.

And then we were free.

I didn't know where we were going to go, or what was going to happen, but wasn't that how I had lived for the past ten years?

The only difference was, now I was with Dan. Wherever we were going, we were going together.

THIRTY-FOUR

We sat in Dan's car in the hospital parking lot. Before we set off, he leaned over to me and gave me a long, slow kiss.

"I was so worried about you," he said. "I thought I was going to lose you, and I couldn't bear for that to happen."

I wasn't used to loving words and romantic gestures. They'd been lacking from my life, and hadn't exactly been part of our relationship up until that point. Maybe what had happened had sparked something inside Dan. Maybe it should also have been a wake-up call for me.

I could have died there at Bittersweet. My mum had, my dad had, I was just repeating the pattern, wasn't I? Instead, I had survived. I was the *final girl* after all.

"I've done what I can at the house," he said.

"Bittersweet?" I don't know what I expected, but I didn't think we would be going back there. Not after everything.

Dan frowned. "Of course, Bittersweet. I've had a new boiler put in, and a CO alarm, just in case. And, um, I bought us a bed. I

229

didn't want to go on and replace all the furniture. I mean, it's your family's, it's yours… but…"

"That's fine," I said. I didn't know how to feel about anything that he was saying. Bittersweet? Again?

"So, you're happy to go back there? It's your home. I just assumed that's what we'd do."

I was exhausted by my stay in hospital and the stress of everything that had happened over the previous weeks. There was no fight left in me.

By replacing the boiler, Dan had got rid of the danger. There would be no more tapping noises, no more hallucinations, no more sleepwalking, no more notes. There would be Dan and me building a future, which is what I had agreed to, wasn't it?

"Okay," I mouthed, quietly.

Dan unclipped his seatbelt and turned his body to face me.

"If you don't want to do this, we can stay somewhere else for a while; we can look for somewhere else to live."

I shook my head.

Dan had been through so much with me, and he still wanted to be with me. If he had seen me at my worst, and was still determined to make a go of things, then how could I refuse him?

Bittersweet was safe now, wasn't it?

And we were together.

Maybe we would only stay there until we had renovated, but maybe we would make Bittersweet our home.

I hadn't ended up like Mum and I wasn't going to.

"I want us to be together. Let's do this," I said with all the enthusiasm I could muster.

I gave Dan a smile that took all of my energy, and he rewarded me with a kiss.

"We're doing the right thing," he said, fastening his seatbelt again, and slipping the car into gear.

I lacked his certainty, but I believed in Dan, and I believed that my future was with him.

It was only a fifteen minute drive across town to the gate of Bittersweet Acres, but all the way there I could feel the adrenaline surge through my body. I was dizzy with a cocktail of fear, anticipation, and excitement by the time we arrived.

Dan must have picked up on my heightened emotional state, because after I got out to let us through and sat back down next to him, he paused.

"Are you sure about this?" he asked.

I wasn't. Of course I wasn't, but I was there, and there was no going back. I'd gone that far. I'd made it through everything Bittersweet had thrown at me.

"As sure as I'll ever be," I said, with a laugh that I knew must have sounded fake. What did he expect, though?

Dan laid his hand on my thigh and gave it a quick squeeze.

"That's my girl," he said.

Then, he turned his gaze ahead, and we set off towards our home.

As we drove up the hill, I saw Bittersweet loom up before us once more.

There was something different about it; it took me a few moments to work out what it was, but then it hit me: the bars were gone from the windows.

"What do you think?" Dan asked, looking over at me. "She looks much better now, doesn't she?"

"She?"

He shrugged. "Bittersweet's been an important character in your life. I've been getting to know her while you've been away."

"Bittersweet tried to kill me," I half-joked. It was too soon for it to really feel funny. "I'm not sure I'm ready to make friends yet."

It was the second time I'd gone back against my better judgement, the second time Dan had talked me around. Still, after all the accusations I'd made, I owed him something.

Was that why I was going back? Was that enough reason? I *owed* Dan?

No. I didn't owe it to Dan. I didn't owe it to Mum. I owed it to myself.

I deserved the future that I had suffered for.

I deserved to make something of myself, and to make something of Bittersweet.

THIRTY-FIVE

Without the bars on the windows, Bittersweet felt more alive. Not alive as in a sentient being that was trying to poison me, but alive as in it no longer felt like a tomb. It was almost Christmas; the days were short, and the darkness came early, but still Bittersweet was lighter than it had ever been.

I stood in the living room and took a deep breath.

"You're safe now, El," Dan said. He slipped his arms around me and held on to me as I let my heart rate settle.

"Thank you," I said. "Thank you for everything."

"Hey, that's okay. That's just what people do for each other. I know you've been through a lot, and probably so much more than I know about, but you're safe now."

I nodded against his chest.

"I want to be more than safe. I want to be happy."

"And you can be. You will be." He lifted my chin and kissed me firmly on the lips. "We will be."

We stood there for some time in silence, both lost in our embrace.

The room around us was the same old living room. The sofa and armchairs were the same ones that I had sat on with my family, the same that I had shared with Dan only days before, but they felt different. Everything felt clean and fresh. The fog in my mind had been lifted, not just with the flushing of the carbon monoxide from my system, but something else had happened to me. I was seeing everything through a new, more positive filter.

I was a survivor. Not just once, but twice now. I was a survivor.

"Listen," Dan said eventually, as we let go of each other. "There's no rush for you to go back to work. Why don't you take some time off, let things settle?"

"Settle?" I tilted my head, considering the word. "Well, I don't suppose they'll want me back at my placement now. I could give it a week until I ask for somewhere else."

I'd never thought of taking a break. I'd worked constantly since I first moved out of Bittersweet. I'd always needed to make money to survive. I was independent and proud of it.

"There's no rush, El. We don't have to pay rent here. I can cover the bills for a while. Let's just make sure you're okay."

It seemed like a sensible suggestion, and after all, Bittersweet was my house. Letting him pay the bills for a month didn't seem like such a bad thing.

"Okay," I agreed. "Just for a couple of weeks, maybe."

The bottom line was that I wanted to believe in him. I wanted to believe that the world could be more sweet than it was bitter.

I would give it a couple of weeks. Long enough to be sure the headaches and sleepless nights were behind me, and long enough to decide what kind of life could be ahead.

Dan brushed a stray curl from the side of my face and said, "I love you."

Rather than reply, my mind flashed back to a time in this very room, years ago, when Dad had done the same thing.

That same gesture. The same words.

I hadn't seen what happened between Mum and him, but I'd heard it. The yelling upstairs, the sobbing. The key turning in the lock. I wasn't long home from school and I'd missed the run-up to the main event. I didn't know what he thought she'd done wrong that time, and really it didn't matter. If the bottle had spun him into one of those moods, there was no escaping, even on our best behaviour.

Mum was shouting, but not for herself. I could hear the words clearly: "Leave her alone. You leave her alone."

All she cared about was keeping me safe. That was all she ever cared about.

Dad stepped back, a surprised look replacing the angry blur, when he walked into the living room and found me standing there.

Without a pause, he leaned towards me, and I braced for impact. I expected to be dragged upstairs and placed in my own cell, but that's not what happened. What happened was worse.

Dad put his arms around me and rested his head against my shoulder.

"I love you, Ella. I love you," he said.

I couldn't stop the instinctive reply.

"I love you too, Daddy."

As soon as I spoke and felt his grip tighten in response, I felt the bile in my throat. I was a traitor to my mum. She was up there, locked away, and I was there, free, in his embrace, betraying her with my actions and my words.

I let her down, and I suppose in part I always blamed myself for not being stronger, not being able to save her.

I wanted Bittersweet back for the both of us. I wanted retribution for how I had let her down, and how I had let myself down. After everything that had happened since I moved back, I was still dangling from that strand of hope that I could find a happy life.

"I love you," Dan repeated, and finally I replied.

"I love you, too."

THIRTY-SIX

So, I gave Bittersweet a couple of weeks. Those weeks turned into a month, and that month crept out into longer.

I found myself in an endless cycle of packing lunches, making dinners, cleaning Bittersweet and caring for Dan. I'd never intended to become a housewife, but there I was, embracing the role.

As we headed into the new year, I started to wonder whether I would ever go back to work. Maybe I didn't have to trudge through a series of shitty jobs to prove anything to anyone, let alone myself. Maybe I could just let someone love me and take care of me. Hadn't I earned that? Wasn't I worthy?

I barely left the acres that Bittersweet was named for. If I was bored during the day, a walk up and around the chicken shed and the stable block was enough to give me time to clear my head. The ground had been hard, and even the mud had been frozen over for most of the time since we moved in.

Then, one day as I headed up towards the buildings in the top field, I saw the first sign of spring: a single snowdrop had burst its way up through the earth, escaping from the shell-like prison of the ground.

"Well done, little one," I smiled, actually saying the words out loud as I crouched to touch the vivid green leaves.

That's what life had become: finding joy in the simple things.

My relationship with Dan was turning out to be one of them. There was more light and less darkness. Was I finally happy?

Despite the softening of the ground, there was a chill in the air, and when I got back to my feet, I thrust my hands deep into my coat pockets.

The fingers of my right hand brushed against something, and I stopped dead. I already knew what it was. Before I let my grip tighten on the scrap of paper, before I pulled it out, I knew.

It was a scrap of paper, just like the ones I'd found when I first moved back to Bittersweet. The ones I had written to myself in my sleepwalking daze.

The note was folded in half, and I held it up, looking at it, trying to work out what it meant. I wasn't trying to guess what was written on it, I could find that out easily enough. What I was wondering was what it meant that there was another note, after all that time.

Taking a deep breath, I opened the paper and read what was written on the other side.

It wasn't that looping scrawl I had written when I was intoxicated by the carbon monoxide. This note was printed, neatly, in my own regular handwriting.

There was only one word.

Trapped.

I stared at the scrap for a few seconds and then I turned back, looking towards Bittersweet down the hill behind me. Its bars were gone, and Dan and I had been working to turn it into our home, but I never left the limits of the acres anymore. There was no need to.

There were no more bad landlords, no more bad jobs.

And there was Dan.

There's more than one way to keep someone a prisoner, I thought.

Then I shook my head, and let the thought float away on the spring breeze.

If I was trapped, I was trapped in a life that I had chosen.

I wasn't locked in a room like a modern-day Rapunzel; I was settled into a life that I had never imagined that I could live. A life where I was loved.

I screwed the note up into a ball and threw it as far away from me as I could.

Then I turned back up the hill, back to the outhouses and the walk that I made every day.

And I carried on.

Dear Reader,

Thanks for choosing Gaslight.

If you enjoyed this book, please leave a review on Amazon, Goodreads, or wherever you share the books that you love.

Reviews help readers to find my books and help me find new readers.

Don't forget that you can visit my website for updates, offers and a free book at:

http://jerowney.com/about-je-rowney

Best wishes

JE Rowney

Printed in Great Britain
by Amazon